Richard coul
emotions chur

This was more than ~~simply~~ to make love to a desirable woman. But how could he convince someone who'd been badly hurt before that she could dare trust again? Even as Jane looked at him now, he could tell that she was worrying about something. She had that far-away expression that told him she daren't commit herself.

Richard lowered his head, longing to kiss her, to soothe away some of the pain he saw in her eyes.

There was a sound of a trolley behind them. He straightened up and continued walking. It would take time and patience to gain Jane's trust. But he was already formulating a plan...

Margaret Barker pursued a variety of interesting careers before she became a full-time author. Besides holding a BA degree in French and Linguistics, she is a Licentiate of the Royal Academy of Music, a State Registered Nurse and a qualified teacher. Happily married, she has two sons, a daughter, and an increasing number of grandchildren. She lives with her husband in a sixteenth-century thatched house near the East Anglian coast.

RELUCTANT PARTNERS

BY
MARGARET BARKER

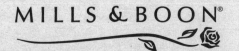

MILLS & BOON®

*MILLS & BOON and MILLS & BOON with the Rose Device
are registered trademarks of the publisher.*

*First published in Great Britain 2001
Harlequin Mills & Boon Limited,
Eton House, 18-24 Paradise Road, Richmond, Surrey TW9 1SR*

© Margaret Barker 2001

ISBN 0 263 82658 9

*Set in Times Roman 10½ on 12 pt.
03-0401-49004*

*Printed and bound in Spain
by Litografia Rosés, S.A., Barcelona*

CHAPTER ONE

JANE'S green eyes flashed as she stared defiantly at her father. 'You can't make me work with this man!'

Dr Robert Crowther gave an exasperated sigh as he ran both hands through his short, sparse, grey hair.

'I can't make you do anything you don't want to. You always were rebellious ever since you were a child! But I'm begging you now to see sense and recognise that Richard Montgomery is absolutely ideal for the practice. If I'd written out a list of requirements for the job, Richard would have met all of them. I can't see what you've got against him!'

Can't you indeed? Jane drew in her breath to prevent herself from saying something she might regret. Her father wouldn't understand her objections even if she told him.

'I think Patricia Drayton was equally well qualified for the job,' she said, outwardly composed but inwardly boiling with indignation.

Why couldn't her father realise she was a thirty-year-old, fully qualified and experienced doctor who was sick of being dictated to? His attitude towards her hadn't changed since he used to tell her off for sneaking into his surgery to play at doctors when he'd been out on his house calls.

She had a sudden fleeting memory of the time he'd returned unexpectedly and had caught her trying to take her teddy bear's blood pressure with his sphygmomanometer. But after he'd torn her off a strip she'd persuaded him that he'd needed his own blood pressure measured. Having watched him do it so many times, and having asked all the questions she'd been able to find time for, she'd understood perfectly how to put on the cuff, pump up the column of mercury and then listen for the bleeps which had indicated the pressure of the blood when the heart had been at rest and when it had been doing one of its regular beats.

Her father's blood pressure had temporarily rocketed sky high, she remembered, so she'd advised him to calm down, as only a wise little eight-year-old daughter could have done. And to give him his due, he'd taken her advice. He'd even, grudgingly, told her that she'd probably make a good doctor. Yes, Dad's bark was worse than his bite but the barking bit was certainly beginning to drive her up the wall!

Her father gave a derisive snort. 'The fact that you and Patricia were at medical school together wouldn't have anything to do with your choice, would it?'

'It would have helped,' Jane conceded quietly. 'We get on like a house on fire.'

Plus the fact that Patricia was female and therefore wouldn't cause any of the complications she'd suffered in the past. For the last four years, since her most recent disillusionment, she'd decided that the less she had to deal with men and their devious demands, the better!

Robert Crowther frowned at his daughter. 'I'm sure you and Patricia do get on well, but she was quite open about the fact that this could only be a temporary appointment. She's planning to join her fiancé in London in a couple of years when they get married, so we would find ourselves having to go through all this again. On the other hand, Richard Montgomery would be fully committed to us. He could live in the flat and—'

'Dad, nobody's lived there for years!'

'What's the state of the flat at the moment, Mrs Bairstow?' Robert Crowther asked the plump, rosy-cheeked, middle-aged woman who had just entered the sitting room, carrying a tray of coffee and home-made biscuits.

Jane moved quickly across the room to take the heavy tray from their housekeeper. She could hear her puffing already from the exertion of carrying the tray from the kitchen and secretly planned to talk her into another health check-up. Basically, Betty Bairstow needed to lose some weight, but her love of cooking, and sampling the end products of her labours, meant that there was very little chance that she'd take any notice of Jane's advice.

Jane set the tray down on a low table by the fire. Settling herself on the edge of one of the fireside chairs, she busied herself with the cafetière and cups as she focused on the problem of finding another partner for the practice. There was still time to reverse her father's decision. All of the six applicants who'd been called for interviews were still waiting for replies. She looked up at Mrs Bairstow who'd been the only mother figure in her life since her own mother had died when she'd been thirteen.

'The flat's in a dreadful state, isn't it, Mrs Bairstow?' she said hopefully, her eyes pleading to get the message across that she wanted this disastrous idea to be knocked on the head.

The housekeeper frowned. 'Nothing I couldn't put right with a few hours' elbow grease, Jane. And you could help me by moving out some of the junk you've kept dumping there. All those old school books that no-body will ever look at again and—'

'I'll do it as soon as I've got some spare time—whenever that might be.' Jane pulled a wry face.

Mrs Bairstow gave her an affectionate smile. 'I know you've been busy since your father had to stop work so I'll be patient. I'll clean around the books but—' She broke off as the implications of the situation sank in. 'Is that young doctor going to move into the flat, then?'

Elizabeth—Betty for short—Bairstow had been an honorary member of the family since she'd taken over from Jane's mother, and she was always the first to find out if changes were in the air. She'd overheard Dr Crowther singing Richard Montgomery's praises the previous week and had already guessed that he'd be the chosen one.

Jane glanced across at her father and gave a resigned shrug. 'I've no idea.'

Through the mullioned windows she caught sight of a black two-seater car approaching fast up the drive. Trust Rick Montgomery to have a flash car! Curiosity was getting the better of her as she stood up and walked nonchalantly over to the window. He certainly cut a dash as he stepped out of the driving seat. How on earth would the patients react when he went out on house calls? The neighbouring farmers would soon cut him down to size and the muddy farm tracks would play havoc with the shiny black surface!

'Dr Montgomery has arrived,' she said quietly, her eyes still riveted on the tall, athletic figure moving purposefully up the front steps.

'I'll go and let him in,' Mrs Bairstow said, handing a cup of coffee to Dr Crowther. 'Don't forget to take your heart pills, Doctor.'

Jane turned round with a pang of guilt. She was the one who should make sure her father remembered his morning pills, but it was invariably Mrs Bairstow who nagged him at coffee-time. Since his heart attack six months ago, there had been so many changes forced on the practice that it was difficult to give her full attention to her father.

Fondly, she looked at him as he composed himself ready to meet the candidate of his choice, determined to make Jane do it his way—as she always did in the end! But she didn't like to give in without a fight. She'd said her piece, she'd made a stand, but she was well aware that it wasn't going to do any good. And she had to concede that having a second doctor on the premises would be better for the patients. She didn't want to have to use the Moortown Deputising Service more than was absolutely essential. The patients objected when they couldn't get the doctor they were used to.

Over the past six months, since her father's enforced retirement, Jane had been the only doctor at the Highdale Practice, and the deputising service had been invaluable. But all that would change now with the appointment of another doctor.

'Dr Montgomery,' Mrs Baistow announced importantly from the sitting-room door. 'In you go, sir.'

Dr Crowther was struggling to his feet, his hand outstretched in welcome. 'Richard! Good to see you again.'

As Jane held herself back, she had an almost surreal experience. She felt as if she were back in medical school at Moortown General, in her first year, and this handsome man in his final year was looking at her in such a sexy way that her legs felt as if they were turning to jelly. It was the devastatingly blue eyes that affected her. She'd never seen anything like them either before or since she'd known him.

With an effort, she pulled herself together. Rick Montgomery wasn't going to make a fool of her again!

'Do sit down, Dr Montgomery,' she said, in what came out as an imperious tone.

She hadn't meant to sound quite so fierce. It wasn't often she felt overawed by someone and the experience was putting her at a disadvantage. She was determined to keep the upper hand if the inevitable happened and she had to work with this man.

She turned her back on him as she picked up the cafetière. 'How do you take your coffee?'

'Black, no sugar.'

Richard sank down into one of the comfy, faded, flowery, cretonne-covered armchairs and watched Dr Jane Crowther pouring coffee into a cup.

My God, she was a cold individual! She'd scared the living daylights out of him last week at the interview, whereas her old man had been positively genial. It was obvious she didn't approve of him so why had they asked him back? She was the one he would be working with since poor old Dr Crowther's cardiac problems had forced him to retire. Maybe they'd asked him over to soften the blow. Bad news over the telephone was always harder to take.

The room had gone ominously quiet, apart from the tinkling of the teaspoons Jane Crowther was fiddling with. She was taking her time! Why didn't she turn round and say something? The suspense of not knowing was unbearable. He'd set his heart on this job. But since meeting the ice maiden he would have to work with he wasn't so sure, so he wouldn't be completely gutted if he hadn't got it.

He stared into the fire. Although it was April there was a keen nip in the air up here in Highdale, and he approved of the fact that they were keeping the ailing Dr Crowther warm. He glanced around the comfortable, well-cared-for but slightly shabby room. The cushion beside him had been lovingly patched with material that didn't quite match. It hadn't changed since that day he'd come here as a child with his mother for a church funds tea-party which Mrs Crowther had organised. His mother had been guest speaker, he remembered. He must have been about ten. There had been a naughty toddler and a boisterous, bossy girl of about five...

'Your coffee, Dr Montgomery.'

He came back to the present as he took the cup from Jane's hands. No, she hadn't changed either! She'd slopped coffee into his saucer. Probably because her hands were trembling. Only ever so slightly, but enough to tell him she was as nervous as he was.

'Do you think we could all get on first-name terms now?' Jane's father said quietly. 'After all, as you're going to be working here, Richard—' He broke off in embarrassment.

Jane raised an eyebrow. Trust Dad to jump the gun! He'd obviously forgotten they hadn't formally offered him the job, and waited for a formal acceptance.

Richard dumped his cup and saucer down on the nearest table with a loud clatter, spilling more of the coffee into the saucer. The devastating blue eyes he turned towards Jane held an enigmatic expression. He certainly didn't look pleased at the premature announcement.

She swallowed hard. Maybe he didn't want the job after all. The room had gone ominously quiet. They were all waiting for Jane to speak. It was up to her to clarify the situation.

She cleared her throat. 'My father would like you to be the new partner if you're agreeable, Richard,' she said carefully, putting a slight emphasis on his name.

He hesitated. It was patently obvious that Jane's father

approved of him, but what about madam? Why was she being so hostile? He took a deep breath. She would be a challenge and he liked challenges! And, after all, it was the patients he would be working with more than her. He could always drive out over the fells on a house call whenever he needed to get away from the dragon!

'I shall be delighted to accept the position,' he said, in his most professional-sounding voice.

'Good, then that's settled.' Robert smiled across at his daughter.

Jane attempted a smile but her lips felt as if they were frozen. She had to go along with the charade, pretend to make Richard welcome. After all, according to his CV he was a very good doctor and that was what her patients needed. The people in this neck of the woods had experienced a rough ride over the last six months. Hadn't they all?

'You'll stay for lunch, won't you, Richard?' said the genial host.

Richard hesitated. Since coming back home to his parents' farmhouse, he'd had to get used to the enormous Yorkshire breakfasts and wasn't sure he could cope with lunch. Especially if Lady Jane was going to be glowering at him across the table.

'Well...'

'Of course you will,' Jane said quickly, maintaining her plastic, dutiful smile.

She couldn't think what had made her endorse the idea. Perhaps she was simply wanting to get to know him better. After all, the ice had to be broken somehow if they were to work together. But only to the extent that they formed an efficient professional relationship. Anything else...

She tried to make herself feel appalled at the idea of

forming a non-professional relationship with Richard but had to admit that, unfortunately, he could still make her feel interested in him as a man. But even if she did want to pursue that line—and she certainly didn't—she wouldn't have a chance with the worldly-wise, sophisticated, much-travelled man he'd become. She couldn't think why he'd described himself on his CV as having no ties. Probably between girlfriends.

She remembered how all the girls had swarmed around him like bees round a honeypot—herself included, unfortunately! But not after she'd found out what he'd really been like. No, she'd had the sense to give him the cold shoulder after that.

The door opened again. 'Mrs Smithson's waiting in the surgery, Dr Jane,' Mrs Bairstow announced, rubbing her damp hands on her apron. 'Says the car wouldn't start this morning so that's why she's late.'

'Late!' Jane glanced at the clock. 'Surgery finished an hour ago.' She stood up. 'OK, tell her I'm coming.'

Her father smiled at her affectionately. 'That's my girl.' He glanced at Richard. 'The folk who live around Highdale have always felt they had the right to disturb us twenty-four hours a day. And when we tried to introduce an appointments system for the surgery it was a complete disaster! We had to go back to the old system of first come first served.'

Jane nodded resignedly. 'That's why they got up that petition when the medical powers that be suggested we should be closed down and merged with the Moortown surgery. I suppose we should be grateful for our patients' loyalty.'

'Nothing's changed since my father ran this surgery,' Robert Crowther said proudly. 'I expect, one day, in the interests of efficiency, we'll have to join forces with the

Moortown doctors, but by then many of the old-timers will have left the fells and gone to live in the town anyway. But in the meantime...'

Jane felt a lump at the back of her throat. She loved Highdale House and the Highdale Practice as much as her father did. She paused by the door and looked back into the room.

'You know, sometimes I wish I hadn't been born into this long line of doctors, and then I go out and deliver a baby, or ease the pain for someone with arthritis, and I think, no, I wouldn't change a thing.'

She gave herself a mental shake. That had been pure sentimentality and it wasn't the image she was trying to portray. She closed the door and hurried down the hall towards the surgery.

Richard stared at the closed door. So the ice maiden wasn't as icy as he'd imagined. Positively human! At the back of his mind he kept having a mental image of a much younger version of this paragon. Hadn't she been in the first year at medical school when he'd been doing his finals?

He struggled hard to remember, but that part of his life was still shrouded in mist, blanked out by the oblivion that had, mercifully, settled over him when he'd had to come to terms with tragedy. He had a sudden fleeting memory that she'd been his friend Simon's girlfriend. Yes, that was it. But she'd been a lively character as far as he remembered. Not this staid, severe, spinsterish...

'I think this calls for a drink, don't you?' Dr Crowther interrupted his thoughts. 'Will you do the honours, Richard? There's a decanter over on that table by the wall.'

'A bit early for me, sir...er, Robert.'

'Well, how about a dry ginger or something equally innocuous, and you can imagine the whisky?'

Jane hurried into her consulting room. 'Hello, Fiona. How are you?'

She sat down at the side of her patient and made a rapid appraisal of the situation whilst she listened to what Fiona had to say. Jane had known her since they'd been children together at the primary school in Highdale village but she hadn't seen much of her since she'd married a farmer and gone to live over in the next dale. Fiona wasn't the sort of woman who was constantly phoning the surgery over minor ailments. But, looking at her today, she didn't appear to be in her usual good health. Definitely on the pale side, and the dark shadows under her eyes showed she hadn't been sleeping enough.

Fiona pushed her bedraggled hair out of her eyes. 'It's this backache, Jane. It's really getting me down. I couldn't get out of bed this morning and Dave had to do the milking all on his own, which didn't please him.'

'Let me have a look at you,' Jane said gently, helping her patient up onto the couch.

During the course of the examination Jane was able to elicit all the information she needed to make a provisional diagnosis. Fiona was only too willing to talk about all the other symptoms that were bothering her.

Jane sat on the edge of the examination couch when she was satisfied she'd got all the information she needed and looked down at her patient.

'You say you couldn't get through to me so you phoned the deputising service a couple of weeks ago because the pain was worse than usual. Did you tell the doctor about all the other things you've told me?'

Fiona was struggling to sit up, wrapping the blanket

around her. Jane plumped up a pillow and put it behind her head.

'I couldn't talk to him like I can talk to you, Jane—you know, all the embarrassing bits. So I just told him about the backache and he gave me some painkillers. He didn't even have time to examine me. Said he had another call to make, and I felt quite relieved really.'

She broke off for a few seconds. 'I mean, I couldn't tell a complete stranger I'd been hoping to start a baby and I'd got all excited when my tummy started swelling, but then my period came and—'

'Well, you've told me now, so don't worry, Fiona,' Jane said gently. She drew in her breath. This was going to be a bit of a shock for her patient. 'I'm going to phone Moortown General and ask them to take you in to give you a further check.'

'When?'

'Today. You need to be seen by a specialist who will check out that lump in your tummy. Where's Dave?'

'He's having a look round your garden. He needed a cigarette. What do you think is wrong with me?'

Jane hesitated. She was always honest with her patients but sometimes she had to wrap it up a bit. 'I think that swelling might be due to some kind of cyst in your stomach. We need to check out what kind of cyst it is and possibly—I only say possibly, Fiona—the specialist may decide to remove it.'

One step at a time. Don't give the patient any more than they can digest at the moment, as her old professor of gynaecology used to say.

Whilst Fiona was dressing, Jane phoned the hospital and made all the arrangements. As she replaced the receiver she thought, Good old Moortown General!

Whenever she had an emergency patient they never let her down.

'Sorry I'm late. Fiona Smithson had a bigger problem than I anticipated.'

Jane sank down into her usual place at the dining table to the right of her father. She looked across the table at Richard Montgomery who was already tucking into his potato and leek soup. He had the grace to put down his spoon and give her one of his devastating smiles which revealed strong white, perfectly formed teeth. She tried her best not to melt, and under the strain found herself scowling at him.

'I'm sorry we started without you, my dear,' her father said, in his polite we-have-a-guest-so-don't-start-getting-argumentative voice.

Mrs Bairstow had rushed from the kitchen, bearing the huge, willow pattern soup tureen.

'I kept it hot for you,' she said, as she filled Jane's soup plate.

The steam was rising and causing Jane's eyes to water, not to mention making her face damp and shiny. It was a good thing she hadn't put on any make-up this morning! Out of the corner of her eye she could see Richard observing her over the top of his spoon. She wished fervently that she'd taken the time to call into the downstairs loo and repair the damage to her face and hair. A comb, a dab of powder and a swipe of lipstick would have bolstered her confidence. She felt a complete mess.

She glanced down at her woollen skirt. It didn't look so bad when she was sitting down but she knew it was too baggy at the back when she stood up.

'So what was the problem?' her new partner asked, in a laconic voice.

Jane took a gulp of her soup. Wow, that certainly was hot! But she was so hungry! It had been a long time since breakfast and she wished, with all her heart, that her father hadn't invited a guest for lunch when she simply felt like slobbing around instead of standing on ceremony. The debonair, impeccably turned out Richard Montgomery was the last person in the world she wanted to have sitting opposite her at this exact moment.

'I mean the problem with your patient?' he persisted. 'Was it serious?'

She was used to discussing her more difficult medical cases with her father over their family meals but she wasn't sure she wanted to talk about it with Richard. For a few seconds she deliberated as to whether it was completely ethical and reluctantly came up with the answer that as he was her partner they had to pool their ideas on all their patients. Fiona might easily become Richard's concern if Jane wasn't around next time she needed medical help.

She took another large spoonful to stem the pangs of hunger before looking across the table. 'My patient had increasing abdominal girth, pressure on her bladder, causing a certain amount of frequency, irregular menstruation, constant pain in the lower back and—'

'Ovarian cyst?' Richard queried.

Smarty pants! He might at least have given her the credit for her diagnostic powers. She wiped her mouth with her napkin before replying.

'Well, that's my provisional diagnosis.'

He was nodding approvingly, curse him!

'So, will you be sending her to…?'

'She's on her way to Moortown General,' she cut in curtly. 'It's all in the notes, in case you have to deal with her when I'm not here. Her name is Fiona Smithson.'

Jane stood up and began to clear the soup plates. Walking behind Richard's chair, she leaned across to take his plate. Her hand brushed against the smooth texture of his sports jacket and she noticed he'd dressed like the country squire today. She had to concede that it suited him. Why did he have to look so handsome when she was trying to dislike him? There was a distinctive aroma of expensive aftershave still lingering around him. She drew back, reacting as if he were a snake who might bite her.

Oh, God! She was already bitten—or was it smitten? She had been ever since she'd passed him on the stairs at Moortown General and her legs had almost packed in and refused to carry her any further. It had been right beside the stone bust of Alexander Fleming and she could have sworn he'd winked at her as she'd passed— Alexander Fleming that was, not Richard!

No, Richard had continued on his way down without a backward glance. At the top, she'd turned and peeped over the banister to see if this apparition from heaven was real or a figment of her highly imaginative, adolescent mind.

He'd paused at the bottom, his hand on the end of the curved banister, and had looked up at her. She remembered, vividly, the intense blush that had spread across her cheeks.

'Are you going to bring those plates, Jane, or shall I come and collect them?' Mrs Bairstow said calmly as she pushed open the door.

History was repeating itself as Jane hurried over to the door, anxious to hide her pink, flushed face from Richard's observant eyes. She took the plates to the kitchen and paused for a moment, leaning against the sink as she looked out through the open kitchen window.

'It's very hot for April, don't you think, Mrs Bairstow?'

'Haven't noticed it myself, dear, but, then, you've been rushing around, haven't you?' the older woman said in a kindly voice. 'Now, if you'd just like to mash those potatoes for me, we'll…'

The men were deep in conversation about the treatment of ovarian cysts when Jane got back to the dining room. They certainly seemed to get on famously with each other. Well, that would help when she felt like bewailing the fact that circumstances had thrown her together with Richard, even though she'd vowed she'd never speak to him again.

When the shepherd's pie had been demolished and the plate of apple dumplings cleared, Robert said he was going for his afternoon nap.

'Doctor's orders,' he said, pulling a wry face. 'Henry Gregson can be the very devil when you're unfortunate enough to be his patient.'

Jane smiled. 'Dad, you chose him as your cardiologist. There are several eminent specialists in the north who—'

'Henry's the best,' her father said grudgingly. 'He was always the clever one when we were at medical school together. Still, I wish he wouldn't be so damn bossy. Don't forget to show Richard the flat, Jane. I've told him all about it. Too bossy by half is Henry. Comes of always getting his own way…'

He trundled away from the table and Jane could still hear him muttering as he climbed the stairs.

'Would you like some coffee?' Jane became very much aware of her place as hostess.

'I'd love some,' Richard said, with studied politeness. 'But could you let me have a look at the flat first so that

I can make my mind up over coffee? And I'll have thought of all the questions I'll need to ask you by then.'

'Of course.' She stood up. 'It's in quite a state. Mrs Bairstow will sort it out before the weekend so if you do decide to move in...'

They walked across the cobbled courtyard that led to the old stable block. There hadn't been any horses there since her grandfather's day. She led the way up the old stone outside steps to the door that opened into the rooms over the stables which had been converted into a flat.

She fiddled with the key. This old, oversized iron contraption had always been a problem.

He reached across her and put his hand over hers. 'Here, let me do that for you.'

She resented the implication that he was in some way superior to her in a practical sense, but at the same time she revelled in the chance of having another surreptitious sniff of his aftershave and enjoying the sheer male proximity of him. It had been so long since...

My God, she was showing all the signs and symptoms of a sex-starved woman! Steady on, girl! Put up the barriers again!

'I shall be surprised if you consider the flat suitable,' she told him primly, as she led the way into the dusty room. 'It's terribly primitive. Only a very small shower room and the tiniest of bedrooms...'

She flung open the door. Mrs Bairstow must have been in already and left a window open. Miriam, their black and white, three-legged cat was curled up on the duvet.

'Miriam, what on earth are you doing in here?' Jane moved towards the bed. Miriam purred but didn't budge as she held her head up to be stroked. Jane relaxed her severe manner and bent down to give the expected stroke.

Richard was watching her carefully. 'What happened to Miriam's leg?'

Jane frowned. 'We think she must have got caught in a trap somewhere. She came limping home one day and her left hind leg was badly injured and almost completely severed. I had to amputate it and stitch her up. She walks very well on three legs and gets spoiled rotten. We all adore her.'

Richard leaned down and caressed the somnolent cat.

'I'm not surprised.' His fingers inadvertently brushed against Jane's.

She caught her breath. It was as if a current of electricity had scorched her.

'I'll take her back into the house,' she said quickly, to cover the embarrassment she was feeling, convinced that her fleeting sensual experience might have been obvious.

'Please, don't move her on my account. I love cats,' Richard said softly, his long, sensitive fingers still stroking Miriam who was looking up at him with adoring eyes.

Jane raised her eyes to his and revelled in the feeling that she was melting inside. But only for a moment! She willed herself to take on her adopted role again.

It would be so difficult for her if he did decide to move in. But from the way he was talking about not disturbing the cat it seemed as if he was contemplating taking the place. It certainly would make sense to have another doctor on the premises, and a man at that. Physically stronger, more able to defend the property against burglars, drug-crazed marauding gangs… She could think of several reasons why it would be practical for him to move in.

But at the same time, the thought of having Richard just yards away from her own bedroom sent shivers down her spine. How would she cope with that? It was only their first day and already she was letting down her guard. She glanced around. The place certainly needed a thorough spring-clean. She'd give Mrs Bairstow a hand when she could find time—perhaps she'd go into Moortown and buy some new curtains for the bedroom. These were practically falling to bits.

That was, if Richard decided he wanted to live here.

'Well, you've probably seen enough,' she said briskly. 'Let's go back and have some coffee.'

CHAPTER TWO

'I'M DYING to hear all about the new doctor, Jane. Tell me, is he as good-looking as everybody says he is?'

Listening to the inquisitive tone in her sister's voice, Jane was beginning to wish she hadn't called in to see her that morning. She might have known she would have to face a barrage of questions about Richard.

She crossed the stone-flagged floor of Caroline's kitchen and leaned against the kitchen table.

'It's ages since you came to see me,' her sister said. 'I was beginning to think you were avoiding me. What made you drop in today?'

'Oh, just an impulse I had. I was on my way back from seeing a patient and…'

Caroline narrowed her eyes as she looked across the table at her sister. 'You don't usually do things on impulse. And you've done something with your hair!'

Jane ran a hand self-consciously over her hair.

'I washed it this morning in the shower and then used that styling brush you bought me for Christmas.'

Caroline dusted the flour from her hands and began brushing egg yolk over the pie she was making.

'Well, it's an improvement, but you ought to have a good professional cut. It's getting far too straggly. And a few highlights would detract from the mousy colour.'

'Thank you, Caroline. I knew I needed someone to boost my ego this morning.'

Her sarcasm was lost on her sister who carried on relentlessly, 'It's not as if you need to look dowdy. Ever since you and Paul split up—'

'Caroline!' Jane's green eyes flashed dangerously. 'I thought we'd agreed that my disastrous affair with Paul was a closed book. It's history so why do you—'

Her sister raised her hands in the air. 'Sorry! I'm sorry! It just slipped out. I won't mention it again.' She gave Jane a sympathetic smile. 'Kettle's boiling. Have you time for a coffee?'

Jane hesitated. Calling in on her sister between house calls had been another impulse she'd given in to. But she could do without her stirring up memories she was trying to forget. That's what happened when you were impulsive and did things on the spur of the moment without thinking. She'd made a point of giving up impulsive behaviour so whatever was the matter with her?

Perhaps it was the balmy spring weather. She looked out through the narrow, mullioned windows of the ancient farmhouse kitchen. Across the field she could see the spring lambs playing happily in the May sunlight. One of the windows was open and she could smell the lilac tree which had blossomed early this year.

'I'd love a coffee,' she said quietly. 'I'll make it so you can get that pie in the oven. Where's Tom?'

She looked around for signs of her three-year-old nephew but saw that all his toys had been consigned to the play area in the corner of the kitchen.

'Having his morning nap. He's started waking with the dawn chorus. There's a nest of house martins under the eaves by his window and the little blighters make a heck of a racket. He trots into our room all bright-eyed and bushy-tailed so Mark takes him to help with the milking.'

Jane grinned. 'Did you say help or hinder? What time does Mark come in for lunch today?'

'Oh, not for ages yet. We've time for a good old chat. I'm dying to know all about that gorgeous hunk you're working with. Rumour has it that he's the spitting image of Paul Newman in his younger days. He's been here a month and I'm still waiting for an invitation to his wel-come-to-the-practice party. Still, you never were one for the social graces.'

Jane lifted the steaming kettle off the hob of the smoul-dering fire. Summer and winter alike, the fire was never allowed to go out in this huge, high-ceilinged kitchen. Her hand shook as she poured the boiling water over the coffee granules. Did she really want to discuss Richard with her sister? Caroline wasn't the sort of person who would be fobbed off with a superficial account of her new medical partner.

She fixed the lid on the cafetière. 'Dad and Richard have had their own little welcome party several times over. I had to speak to Dad about his alcohol consump-tion but he said it was a temporary lapse because he was so pleased to have another man about the place.'

Caroline closed the oven door on her pie and moved back to the table. 'So Dad and Richard Montgomery get on well together, do they? Well, that will be helpful.'

Jane pushed the plunger down in the cafetière with a resounding thwack. 'What do you mean?'

'I should have thought that was obvious. After all the fuss you made about not choosing a man for the practice, I couldn't believe you'd given in.'

'Dad can be very bossy.'

Caroline laughed and tossed back her long blonde hair. 'So can you! A right chip off the old block you are!'

Jane's mobile started ringing. 'Dr Crowther.'

'It's Richard here, Jane.'

She willed the flush on her cheeks to disappear as she

looked across at her sister who was grinning from ear to ear. Why couldn't it have been a patient? She could have coped with a professional situation in front of her all-seeing sister, but…

'Yes, Richard?'

'I've had a call from a patient by the name of Alan Greenwood.'

'Alan Greenwood has multiple sclerosis. He—'

'Yes, so I see from the notes.'

She could hear the crackle of paper at the other end of the line. Caroline was mouthing something at her but she tried to ignore her sister as she adopted a totally professional expression.

'Alan's not feeling so good today,' Richard continued. 'He's asked if you could go out to his house. He says it's not urgent, this afternoon or tomorrow would be fine, but I thought today would be better. I'd like to go, too, in case I have to deal with him in the future when you're not on duty.'

'I'll come back to the surgery and we'll go and see Alan together in about…'

She was glancing at her watch but her sister was gesticulating and speaking in a stage whisper. 'Ask him round for a coffee. It's on the way to Alan's. Oh, go on, sis, I'm dying to meet him and this would be…'

Jane had already put her hand over the phone. 'He can hear everything you're saying, Caroline, so—'

'Good! Then ask him over, will you?'

Jane took a deep breath. 'I'm actually at my sister's. She wonders if you'd like to meet me here for a quick coffee. It's not far… Oh, you would? Well, turn left when you go out of the gate and follow the road…'

Her sister was grinning from ear to ear as she scooted

out of the kitchen and dashed up the stairs to change into
something more suitable for this exciting occasion.

'This is a pleasant surprise in the middle of a working
morning.' Richard was smiling as he looked across the
kitchen table at the two sisters. How would anybody ever
guess that there was a family connection between these
two?

Jane took a sip of her coffee as she watched Caroline
visibly melting with admiration. She was running a hand
through her long, shiny, blonde hair. In the few minutes
it had taken Richard to drive over, Caroline had discarded
her apron and changed into tight, figure-moulding jeans
and a very sexy, revealing shirt. Jane frowned, although
inwardly she was smiling to herself. Caroline's behaviour
was so predictable! Flirting was an enjoyable pastime to
her—like window-shopping, but completely harmless.
She'd always been a lively girl and, being a housewife,
she jumped at the chance of any excitement to brighten
up the day.

Caroline was smiling now, showing her perfect white
teeth. 'I can assure you, it's an absolute pleasure for me
to be entertaining a handsome young bachelor in my
kitchen.'

She giggled girlishly as she risked a sideways glance
at Jane. 'My sister doesn't approve of me flirting, but one
of the good things about being an old married lady is that
you can get away with it because it's perfectly harmless—more's the pity!'

Oh, she was shameless! Jane glanced at Richard and
could see that he was enjoying himself.

'Not so much of the old! You can't be more than...'

'I'm twenty-seven, three years younger than Jane. And
I've been married since I was eighteen. Seems like a

lifetime. I'd just left school and I was wondering what the…what on earth I was going to do, having failed all my exams. Jane got all the brains from Dad, you see, and there weren't any left when I came along.'

'But my sister got all the beauty from our mother,' Jane put in wryly. 'I was always known as Plain Jane. I wore a brace on my teeth for years and I never had any interest in clothes, like Caroline did.'

She was aware that Richard was watching her intently.

'Anyway, to continue my story,' Caroline put in to cover the sudden silence, 'it was a good thing that Mark came along and whisked me away to be married, because I can't think what else I could have done. Marriage is very fulfilling but sometimes I envy you single ones. All that freedom!'

Richard took a sip of his coffee before clearing his throat. 'I'm not, strictly speaking, a bachelor…' He paused, as if searching for words.

A shiver of something akin to disappointment ran down Jane's spine. He was going to reveal some long-term girlfriend who would muscle in and—

'No, I was married once, but I've been on my own for years.' There was a deep sadness in his voice.

Jane would have liked to know more and she could see that her sister was almost bursting with curiosity. For once she had the good sense to keep quiet. But not for long!

'Are you related to the Montgomerys over in Deepdale?'

He put down his cup and leaned back against the old, wooden carver. 'Sylvia and Desmond are my parents.'

Caroline's eyes widened. 'Wow! Sylvia Montgomery was my role model when I was a child. I've watched all her old films on the telly. Is she still working?'

Richard grinned. 'Mum is currently resting, as it's known in the trade. She'd love to work again but the only parts she gets offered are old lady character parts and she doesn't want to drop the glamorous image yet.'

Caroline moved her chair a little closer to Richard's. 'What was it like, growing up with a film star for a mother?'

'I have to admit I never even thought about it. She was just Mum. I was sent away to school when I was seven so I was only home for the holidays, and even then I was usually packed off to a children's adventure camp or my grandparents' house in Scotland.'

Caroline nodded. 'I suppose that's why you're considered something of a stranger around here. Where were you working before you came back to the Dales?'

'Mostly in hospitals in the Far East but most recently I finished my GP training at a large practice in Leeds,' he replied, in a studiously patient voice.

'What made you change from hospital work to being a country GP?'

Richard put down his cup and glanced at his watch. 'Oh, that's a long story. Far too complicated to go into.'

Jane stood up, anxious to make a move before Caroline started asking any more questions. She sensed that her sister had touched on a raw nerve. 'I think we should go out to see Alan—that's if you're ready, Richard.'

He was on his feet already. Was it her imagination or did he look relieved that the interrogation was over?

'We'll take my car, Jane. We'll pick yours up later,' Richard said, putting a hand under her elbow as they reached the outside door.

Normally, she would have bristled if a man had chosen to touch her in such a familiar way. She usually took it to mean that she was being treated like the little woman who couldn't get herself through a doorway without the help of some superior man. But it was strangely calming to have Richard's fingers under her arm.

No, it was more than that. It was positively sensual. She was glad she'd taken her jacket off because the experience was more tantalising on her bare skin.

Tantalising! Yes, that was it. She was enjoying a tantalising experience with a highly desirable but utterly unobtainable man, and there was absolutely no harm in that.

She drew in her breath as she folded her long legs into the passenger seat of the impossibly-difficult-to-negotiate black sports car. She loved the sleek lines of this stream-lined monster but the designers hadn't thought about the poor passenger who would have to try and look elegant whilst coping with not showing too much as she climbed in.

As usual, because she was doing house calls, she was wearing one of her old woollen suits. This skirt was particularly baggy but it didn't allow for the gymnastics required by this car! She'd always thought her suits went with the image of reliable country doctor. It showed she was a no-nonsense, no-frills sort of get-on-with-the-job type of woman. But during the last couple of weeks she'd begun to wonder if the patients would be less reassured if she really were to, as Caroline put it, smarten herself up.

Getting that hair styling brush out of its packaging at half past six that morning had been a step in the right direction. She tried to smooth down her skirt, brushing at the dog hairs she'd picked up from stroking the exuberantly friendly dog in her last patient's kitchen.

Caroline was waving from the doorway as she looked back. 'Give me a call and tell me...'

Fortunately, whatever it was that her sister wanted her to tell was drowned in the engine noise. It could have been something really embarrassing! There was no way of stopping her irrepressible sister, Jane thought affectionately.

She glanced sideways at Richard and felt a flutter of butterflies flying around in the pit of her stomach. My God, he was handsome! What had she done to deserve this tantalisation? This constant reminder of the untouchable? She wasn't going to get her fingers burned again— not if she could help it! But surely it would do no harm to look and give herself the pleasure of admiring him from afar.

Richard took one hand off the wheel and placed his fingers lightly on her arm. She'd had the common sense to put back her jacket so his fingers didn't unnerve her quite so much this time. Even so, there was a kind of tight feeling in her chest.

'You're very quiet, Jane,' he said, as he put his hand back on the wheel.

She breathed more easily. 'It's only because we've been with my sister and you're experiencing the unexpected calm after the storm of non-stop interrogation.'

He threw back his head and laughed.

Oh, what a glorious sound! She loved to hear the deep rich laughter of a desirable man. Maybe that had been her downfall. She'd been a pushover for anyone who'd amused her. She wondered if Richard had the same sense of humour that she did. Slightly zany. She hoped so. Anyway, it would be fun to find out.

He was swallowing his laughter now as he concentrated on the final hairpin bend that led to the top of the moors. A stray sheep, followed by a nervous, bleating lamb, suddenly decided to cross the narrow road. Richard slammed on the brakes, breathing deeply.

'You ought to be teaching your baby about road safety!' he called to the startled sheep.

Jane laughed. 'The sheep code—look left, look right, then charge across anyway, preferably in front of the nearest car. I'm sure the ewes teach their lambs to play chicken. See who can make the most number of cars stop dead in the road without getting hurt.'

Richard restarted the stalled engine and drove onto the moors. As the pace accelerated she could feel the wind in her hair.

She ran her hand over her hair. 'I feel like one of those woolly sheep. Can't think why I bothered to try and tame my hair this morning.'

He glanced sideways. 'Nothing wrong with looking carefree and windswept, but you might like to wear a scarf next time.'

So there was going to be a next time! These combined house calls were going to be a pleasant distraction from her usual routine. Her pulses were racing with exhilaration. She hadn't felt so alive for years. Not since... No, she wasn't going to think about Paul. This feeling was something quite different. In spite of all her misgivings about him, Richard Montgomery had turned out to be the sort of person she might be able to have a real friendship with.

Over the last month as they'd worked together she'd come to admire his professionalism and vibrant attitude to life. She'd been forced to admit to herself that he inspired her. She looked forward to morning surgery when he was around. And it was good to know that there was a man, other than her invalid father, on the premises after it became dark. There were no other houses around for a mile, until the beginning of Highdale village. So it was comforting to know that she would be able to call on Richard in an emergency.

But since he'd moved into the flat, she hadn't disturbed him during his off-duty times. She valued her own privacy so she wasn't going to disrupt Richard's—except for a dire emergency! But the fact that he was only just across the courtyard was a definite source of comfort…and something else…

She'd had to reprimand herself for wondering what it might be like to go up those ancient, uneven, stone steps to the rooms where she used to play as a child and simply call on him, ask him how he was getting on, make some excuse just so she could sit down and chat to him on a one-to-one basis, without being interrupted by her father or the patients.

Well, she had him on a one-to-one at the moment. Driving along, with the wind in her hair, she could almost imagine they were going out on a date together.

At the thought of a date her mood shifted and she came down to earth with a bang. All those years ago at medical school when he'd let her down. He didn't even seem to remember and she certainly wasn't going to remind him. Or was she? Wouldn't it be a good thing to find out exactly why he'd stood her up?

But not yet! Not when they were forming a nice, comfortable, friendly relationship that wasn't going to go anywhere significant. A nice, uncomplicated, platonic…

'You'll have to direct me when we get to the next bend.' His voice broke into her thoughts. 'I studied the map before I left the surgery but…'

'Take a right turn in about half a mile. Alan's road is a bit bumpy so I hope you don't spoil your beautiful car.'

She hesitated. 'It's not the sort of car we've usually had in the practice.'

He smiled. 'Should I take that as a reprimand from my senior partner?'

'No, no! Just a comment.'

He turned off the road and started along a bumpy track. 'I remember the disparaging way you looked at my car on the first day I arrived. If looks could kill, my car would have been shattered into a thousand pieces.'

Jane drew in her breath. 'I'm told I sometimes have that effect on people. I make it quite plain what my opinions are, but I've changed my opinion about your car, Richard.'

'You've changed a lot of things since I first met you,' he said quietly.

'For the better, I hope,' she quipped.

He brought the car to a halt in front of a long, low, ramshackle building and switched off the engine.

'Oh, definitely for the better,' he said in a deep, husky voice.

She felt a sensual shiver run down her spine as she dared to look across at him. He was watching her, almost, she thought, as if he was afraid she might suddenly turn on him and destroy the tender moment. For an instant she felt ashamed of the uncharitable thoughts she'd harboured when he'd first arrived.

'If I was less than welcoming when you first started working at the practice...' she began carefully, but he touched her mouth with a long, tapering, oh, so sensitively seductive finger.

'Responsibility makes people tough and that was your way of coping with a difficult situation. Have you always been the strong one in the family?'

She stared at him. He was leaning across towards her

and she could feel his hot breath on her face fanning the
flames of desire that had sprung up, unbidden, deep down
inside her.

She nodded, mesmerised by those sexy, blue, bedroom
eyes. A woman could drown herself in the depths of
pools like that.

'I was thirteen when Mum died. Dad went to pieces
emotionally. He could cope perfectly well with his professional life but anything else was beyond him. I put a
card in Highdale post office window, advertising for a
live-in housekeeper. Mrs Bairstow moved in to take care
of the domestic side of things but I had to keep the family
ship afloat.'

'And there was no time to be a frivolous teenager,' he
said, his voice husky with tenderness.

'Absolutely not. Not with a grieving father and an im-
possibly naughty sister to contend with.' She paused as
the memories flooded back. 'Although I did rebel for a
while at seventeen. Once I'd made sure that Dad had got
over Mum's death, I dyed my hair different colours to
see if he would notice me.'

Richard put his hand gently on her shoulder. 'And did
he?'

She grinned. 'You bet! But not in the way I'd hoped
for. He practically disowned me during my Picasso period.'

'Picasso?'

'We'd been learning about Picasso's paintings at
school and I was fascinated when the teacher said the
artist had been obsessed by the colour blue for a certain
length of time. It was always referred to as his blue period. So I decided to have my own blue period.'

Richard laughed. 'Besides the blue hair, what else did
you colour?'

Jane pulled a wry face. 'Only my nails, but it was the blue hair my dad objected to and also the weird paintings I stuck on the kitchen walls. I used to spend hours churning out abstract paintings of people with heads larger than their bodies and two eyes on one side of their faces. I thought that if it was good enough for a world-famous artist like Picasso…'

She broke off. Richard was looking at her with that strange enigmatic expression he often held when she was talking. He must be thinking she was mad, talking about her favourite artist as if he were a personal friend!

Richard blinked his eyes. For an instant he could have thought he was listening to Rachel—the same *joie de vivre*, the same passion for art, a zany sense of humour that transcended the mundane. In outward appearance Jane was nothing like Rachel, but inwardly… He gave himself a mental shake. Would he ever get over Rachel and be able to move on with his life?

'Look, we ought to go in and see our patient,' Jane said quickly, unnerved by the way Richard was staring at her. 'He'll be wondering why we're sitting outside.' Hurriedly, she pushed open the passenger door.

Alan was leaning heavily on his stick as he opened the door. 'Good of you to come so quickly. I hope I haven't dragged you away from more deserving patients.'

Jane gave him a reassuring smile. Alan was always so apologetic, so self-effacing. There was no one more deserving of their attention than he was. He was definitely lacking in self-confidence now and that wasn't surprising, considering the way he'd had to cope with his affliction by himself. He was only thirty-five, about the same age as Richard, but he seemed a good ten years older.

She looked around the low-ceilinged living room. It could do with a good clean but Alan had declined all her offers of getting in someone from Social Services to sort out his domestic situation. He'd made it quite plain he didn't want charity.

'So how are you, Alan?' she said, as she sank down into one of the springless armchairs. Her bottom was actually touching the floor. She tried to do a surreptitious wriggle and decided it would be easier to stand up as soon as she didn't have to make her discomfort too obvious. Richard, she noticed, had wisely declined a chair.

She looked around at the shabby, uncared-for surroundings. Heavens, Alan's mother must be turning in her grave! Ever since she'd died, a couple of years ago, the place had been going to rack and ruin and Jane felt powerless to do anything about it. If this was the way Alan wanted to live then she had to respect his wishes. But if or when the multiple sclerosis progressed to the next stage she would have to insist on making some practical arrangements for his welfare.

Her patient was sitting on the one and only wooden chair that still had a cane-bottomed seat on it.

'I've not been so good, actually, Dr Jane,' Alan said carefully. 'I'm getting very stiff. It's getting harder to…to move around. Yesterday I fell over and it took me ages to pull myself up onto my feet again.'

She looked across at Richard, who was rapidly scanning the case notes he'd brought with him.

'I see you haven't yet tried Alan on beta interferon,' he said quietly.

'The last time Alan saw Mr Fairburn, the neurologist consultant at Moortown General, it was suggested we might prescribe it when…when it was necessary,' Jane said carefully, willing Richard to catch her drift. She didn't want to have to spell out the fact that they'd been holding off, hoping that further medication wouldn't be necessary.

Richard nodded understandingly. 'So it looks like a wise course of action, doesn't it?'

Jane nodded before turning to her patient. 'We're going to put you on some new medication,' she said gently.

She would phone James Fairburn when she got back to the surgery and tell him she thought Alan had now reached the stage when beta interferon might slow down the progress of the disease. It should, hopefully, improve his mobility and ease the worry of further falls.

Alan frowned. 'Is it safe?'

Jane looked at Richard.

'There are always possible side-effects with any drug,' Richard said carefully. 'But beta interferon has undergone extensive tests and has proved to be very effective in the majority of cases which have reached the stage you're at.'

'OK, I'll give it a try.'

Richard put a reassuring hand on his patient's shoulder. 'I'll bring some out to you tomorrow morning.'

Jane could hear a car coming up the drive. She heard it stop outside the door and then footsteps coming down the passage. A tall, thin woman in jeans and a hand-knitted sweater came into the room, carrying a bag of supplies from the village store.

'Diane!' Alan's face lit up.

Jane thought she could detect a faint diffusion of pink underneath the non-designer stubble.

She vaguely recognised the young woman who used to work in the grocer's shop in Highdale and remembered that she hadn't been around for a couple of years.

Diane nodded at Jane. 'Hello, Doctor. I've come to give Alan a hand.'

'Diane's been travelling the world,' Alan said, a certain amount of proprietorial pride creeping into his voice. 'She shows me her photographs and tells me all about the places she's been to. It's so interesting!'

'It's going to be even more interesting today because I'm going to make a start on sorting out this pigsty,' Diane said in a dry tone.

'I've told you, I like it the way it is so...'

Diane turned around and started heading for the door. 'Well, if that's your attitude, Alan...'

'I think it would be an excellent idea,' Jane said quickly. 'Alan, you can't expect Diane to spend time with you if she doesn't feel comfortable here. And I don't expect it's easy for you to keep up with the domestic chores, is it?'

Alan shrugged. 'OK, Diane. I'd like you to help,' he said in a resigned tone. 'And I'll try to give you a hand.'

The smile on Diane's face as she turned back into the room helped to soften her rather hard features. 'I should hope you will. If you think I'm going to sort this lot out by myself you've got another think coming.'

Richard put the car into gear and moved off down the bumpy road. Turning round, Jane waved to Diane who was standing in the doorway.

'Can't make out the connection there,' Richard said, gripping the steering-wheel as he negotiated a large pothole in the middle of the road. 'But you know everybody round here so...'

'I've no idea what's going on,' Jane said, leaning back. 'They're about the same age so they may have been friends when they were younger. I don't know if Diane's come back from her travels with some philanthropic idea about helping the less fortunate or—'

'Or maybe they genuinely get on together…as…as friends,' Richard finished off. 'I mean, the strangest people often get together, don't they?'

She sank deeper into the soft leather seat. 'Quite true.'

She and Paul had been like chalk and cheese and yet they'd managed to have an affair. A disastrous affair, she reminded herself. A never-to-be-repeated experience that had left her deeply scarred.

'Alan seems to be genuinely…er, fond of Diane,' she said carefully. 'I hope she won't hurt him. I mean, if she stops coming to see him…'

'I think we should monitor the situation carefully,' Richard said quietly. 'It's one thing to provide the miracle drugs but if his heart really is involved…' He broke off. 'Well, let's look on the bright side. It will be good while it lasts and we'll give him support if we need to help him pick up the pieces.'

'Picking up the pieces is never easy,' Jane said softly.

'You sound as if you speak from experience,' he said evenly.

'Oh, yes.'

He could hardly hear her voice but the underlying pathos touched him more than her words. There was some kind of background sorrow underneath the tough, confident exterior. Here was a woman who had obviously suffered. She'd reached a point of acceptance of her role in life. But it was an acceptance that had dulled her and taken away that spirit of adventure she'd had before she'd been hurt. He felt the inescapable urge to scrape off the outer layer and reach the true person he occasionally glimpsed. This complicated girl intrigued and fascinated him in a way that he had definite reservations about.

He didn't want to become involved. He didn't know whether he was capable of becoming involved again. But he reminded himself that Jane was such an independent character that she wouldn't want involvement anyway.

He'd never been out with a strong, feisty girl who affected him like this. Even Rachel, tough as she had been in her professional life, had always gone along with his every wish. But Jane was uncharted territory, a challenge in every way. Deep down he felt a strong primeval longing to take her in his arms and hold her against him, to feel the soft womanly curves against his body, caress her with such gentle sensitivity that she would want to mould herself against him.

A group of cows was coming towards them in the middle of the road. Richard pulled over onto the grass verge and the farmer walking behind his cattle nodded his approval. He leaned back against the driving seat and realised that he was breathing rapidly and it had nothing to do with meeting up with the herd. He was going to have to get a grip on himself if he was to keep the good working relationship that was developing between them. He didn't want to do anything to spoil the headway they'd made together but at the same time it couldn't do any harm to follow his natural feelings.

'I was wondering if you'd like to come out with me one evening,' he said steadily. 'There's a concert in Moortown next week and—'

'Not in the town hall?' she said quickly.

He was brought back to reality by her startled tone. What was wrong with the town hall?

'Yes, actually, it is in the town hall, but if you—'

'Sorry, it was just something I was... Memories, you know,' she finished off lamely.

So he really didn't remember! She was just one of the many girls he'd encountered during a long lifetime of being hero-worshipped. Oh, well, it couldn't do any harm to stir up a few memories and maybe lay the ghost once and for all. Especially if she jogged his memory! Because she didn't feel she could even begin a friendship until she knew why he'd chosen not to turn up that night, twelve years ago.

'A concert would be lovely,' she said quickly, surprising herself by her enthusiasm.

Richard felt a pang of apprehension. He'd never taken anyone like Jane out before and he had no idea how to approach the situation. Neither had he really any idea why he'd asked her out in the first place. The fact that she intrigued him wasn't enough to sustain him through the evening if she adopted one of her frosty moods with him—as well she might.

But, as he'd reminded himself so often during the past month, Jane was a challenge and he enjoyed challenges!

'We'll drive over in my car, so don't forget your scarf this time,' he said brusquely.

'I won't forget the scarf if you don't forget to turn up,' she said quietly.

He frowned and leaned across to put a tentative hand on her shoulder. Something deep down inside him was urging him to get nearer to this fascinating but enigmatic woman. All he knew was that he wanted to spend more time with her. But it was a bit like approaching a Rottweiler! He never knew when he was going to get bitten!

'What did you mean by that last remark?' he said evenly. 'In the month I've been working with you, have I ever let you down?'

She turned to look at him and allowed herself to drown once more in those wonderful blue eyes. She could feel shivers of real desire mounting up inside her and knew that none of the feelings she'd had for him when she was young had been dulled by the passage of time. In spite of all her unpleasant experiences, if he moved any nearer she would listen to her heart and ignore the sensible inner voice that urged her to remember the past and be a wise girl.

'I wasn't talking about the present day. You've never let me down since we've been working together,' she said softly, desperately aware of the touch of his fingers on her jacket.

If only she'd removed it before getting into the car, she could have nestled closer and...

A car was passing. It was sure to be one of their patients! Inquisitive eyes would be wondering why the two doctors were parked on the grass verge in the middle of nowhere. She moved back towards the passenger window, away from the centre of the car, away from temptation.

But Richard leaned over and gathered her into his arms. 'I haven't a clue what you're talking about,' he said, his voice husky. 'I expect you'll explain what you're on about in your own good time. You usually do.'

Jane looked up into his eyes and saw real tenderness, and at that moment she made a conscious decision to go along with her natural feelings. Slowly he bent his head towards her, his eyes watching her face for any sign of a negative reaction. She held her breath, longing for the touch of his lips. When he kissed her it was like the soft touch of a butterfly's wing.

But she barely had time to savour the moment before it was over. He was already pulling away, the expression in his eyes apprehensive. She wondered whether, if she'd responded more, he would have deepened the kiss.

And how would she have reacted?

CHAPTER THREE

'I'VE got the tickets for the concert.'

Jane looked up from the desk in her surgery as Richard poked his head round the door. She gave him a reserved smile, determinedly ignoring the thudding of her heart. Since he'd kissed her in the car a week ago she'd been pursuing a policy of holding him at arm's length. She'd given herself a mental ticking-off for behaving like a star-struck teenager.

'Tomorrow night, isn't it? I've arranged for the deputising service to take over.'

She was being deliberately professional in her manner. 'Oh, and, Richard...' She pulled out a thick envelope with the case notes of one of her patients. 'There's one more call for you to make this morning. Harry Fielding's arthritis is getting worse. He's taken to his bed but his wife thinks, as I do, that he should get up or he'll seize up completely. You'll need to examine him and make a proper assessment of his condition. I suggest you also check on his painkillers and anti-inflammatory drugs and find out why the physiotherapist hasn't been to see him.'

Richard walked across to the desk and stood looking down at her, a barely concealed expression of amusement on his face. 'I'm so glad you give me advice on our patients. I'd never be able to fathom it out for myself.'

'Sorry!' She apologised before she could stop herself, even though she was still trying to maintain the firm stance of senior partner. 'I just like to fill in the case history for you.'

'And very useful it is, too,' he said, a serious expression returning to his face.

As he leaned over to remove the case notes from her desk she breathed in the heady scent of his aftershave. It was like an aphrodisiac! She could feel herself melting even though it was barely nine o'clock in the morning.

Quite unnecessarily, Jane reached for the notes and handed them to him. Their fingers touched, as she'd hoped they would. She looked up at him to augment the delicious sensations that were stealing over her again.

He touched her cheek briefly, in a highly unprofessional manner. A month ago she would have bristled with indignation but it was impossible to ignore the melting feeling inside her. Ever since he'd kissed her she'd wanted more. So why should she deny herself a harmless flirtation just because she knew it couldn't last?

Richard was already moving away towards the door and she knew she'd once again ignored the sensible voice inside her head that was supposed to help her keep her resolutions. She was sure that the expression in her eyes must have more than hinted that she might not be averse to a little romance.

She sat motionless at the desk after he'd gone, physically unable to start work. As she heard his car drive away she breathed a sigh of relief. She was leaning back in her chair staring into space when Lucy Sugden, her part-time nurse-cum-receptionist came in.

'Fiona Smithson's here. Said she had to come early because she has to go over to Leeds to see her mother.' She broke off. 'You all right, Jane?'

'I'm fine!' Jane put on her brightest smile. The hyper-perceptive Lucy would be jumping to the wrong conclusions. 'Why shouldn't I be?'

'You don't usually spend time daydreaming.'

'I was indulging myself for once,' she said briskly. 'There's a couple of letters here, Lucy. If you could get them done I'll sign them before you go.'

Lucy nodded. 'No problem.'

As the door closed behind her receptionist, Jane knew she hadn't been fooled by her sudden return to efficiency. Lucy had remarked a couple of times over the last week that she approved of the way Jane and Richard were getting on together. She'd hinted at more, but Jane had stopped the conversation at that point. Lucy, in her forties, was always trying to give her the advice of a happily married wife and mother.

Jane knew she was lucky to have someone as professionally experienced as Lucy who found that part-time work was ideal for her situation. A trained nurse, she had given up hospital work before the birth of the first of her three children. When they'd started school she'd taken a part-time secretarial course and had been an absolutely ideal candidate for the work at Highdale Practice.

But since Richard had arrived and thrown Jane's former strategy of dealing with the opposite sex into a state of flux, she'd often wished she didn't have to put up with Lucy's inquisitive but well-meaning remarks.

As soon as Fiona Smithson came in she pulled herself together, relieved that she was able to give her full attention to her patient. Her mind never wandered when she was concentrating on the medical case in hand.

'I'm having a check-up at Moortown General next week, Jane, but I wanted a chat with you first,' Fiona said, settling herself in the chair beside Jane at the front of the desk.

Jane smiled reassuringly. 'So, how are you feeling, Fiona?'

'Relieved you sent me to hospital before it got any

worse. A couple of months ago that locum doctor said I'd probably got indigestion, when all the time I'd got this ovarian cyst growing inside me. I feel a lot better without it, I can tell you.'

'Good, well, if you'd like to get up on the couch I'll have a look at your tummy.'

Jane satisfied herself that the abdominal organs were all back in place after the operation five weeks previously. Without consulting the notes, she remembered that she'd had Fiona admitted to Moortown General on the day Richard had arrived, and the operation had taken place the next day.

'Neat scar,' she observed. 'And your tummy's a lot flatter.'

'I'm hoping to expand it before long,' Fiona said, with a shy grin. 'There isn't any reason why I shouldn't get pregnant, is there?'

Jane hesitated. 'It would be wise to leave it for a few months. After any abdominal operation it takes a while for everything to settle down and function normally.'

'But removing that cyst didn't harm my ovary, did it? I mean, is it still producing eggs that would make a baby?'

'That's what you'll have to ask Mr Thomas when you have your check-up next week,' Jane said gently, referring to Fiona's gynaecologist. 'He'll be able to tell you if that ovary is still functioning normally, but in any case you still have a second ovary that wasn't affected. We'll just have to wait and see.'

She held out a hand to help Fiona sit up.

'Thanks, Jane. It's always good to check things out with you before I have to go to the hospital. It's not that I'm scared of hospitals but...'

Jane patted her hand. 'Come and see me any time, Fiona. That's what I'm here for.'

She was about to reach out and buzz to let Lucy know she was ready for her next patient when her outside phone rang.

She spoke briskly. 'Dr Crowther here… Richard!'

She felt so transparent! Why did he always have to catch her off guard? She'd greeted him as if she hadn't seen him for weeks.

'I'm out at Harry Fielding's place. According to his wife, he refused to see the physiotherapist he had before.'

'Was it Grace Purdy?'

Jane waited as she heard Richard conferring with Mrs Fielding.

'Yes, it was.'

'Ah! Grace is a good physiotherapist but she can be a bit rough with the patients. I'll phone the physiotherapy centre and find someone less exacting. She tends to put their backs up.' She broke off. 'That wasn't meant to be a pun,' she put in hastily. 'I know just the person who'll help Harry and I'll insist that I get no one else but her,' she finished off, emphatically making the point that she wouldn't take no for an answer.

'I'm sure you'll get your own way, Jane.'

Was it her imagination or did she hear him chuckling down the line?

'What's so funny?' she asked sharply.

'You are, but I'm getting used to it.'

Jane put the phone down. How dared he make fun of her! She began to grin as she saw the funny side of it. Maybe she had overdone the power-mad professional voice for Richard's benefit. Wouldn't it be a lot easier if she didn't try to put on an act in front of him?

She sat absolutely still after the call was disconnected.

She could do without all this churning of the emotions. If Richard hadn't come into her world she could have continued with her orderly life.

But wouldn't it have been dull? Jane leaned back in her chair and allowed herself to think about the date she was having tomorrow with him. She knew she was behaving like a star-struck teenager but that was how he made her feel. She'd felt exactly like this the first time she'd gone to meet him at Moortown town hall.

And he hadn't turned up! He'd let her down. She remembered she'd been heartbroken. Why, all these years later, was she giving him another chance? Didn't it just prove, as she'd long suspected, that she was totally naïve where men were concerned? She'd been let down so many times that it seemed inevitable it would happen again. Even if their date went off OK tomorrow, it wouldn't be long before Richard would be moving his attentions to someone more exciting.

Richard parked the car in the large car park next to the town hall and went round to open the passenger door.

Jane gathered her skirts around her and attempted to extricate herself without revealing the ladder in her last pair of wearable tights. It had been Lucy's idea that she should dress up for the occasion and she was regretting it already.

'Everybody dresses up for the concerts at the town hall,' Lucy had told her when, following a chat with Mrs Bairstow, she'd discovered where Jane was going. 'The mayor will be there and there'll be loads of VIPs.'

'Oh, well, that settles it,' Jane had said dryly, and had immediately gone to her room to check that the expensive cream silk suit she'd worn for a wedding had still been wearable.

Looking up at Richard now, she felt sure he was of the same opinion as she was.

'I'm hopelessly overdressed, aren't I?'

He squeezed her hand. 'You look charming, absolutely charming.'

'And hopelessly out of date.'

She wished fervently that she'd ignored Lucy's advice and worn something she felt comfortable in. She had to admit that the idea had been to make Richard feel proud of her as she strolled amongst all the dignitaries. But when had she ever cared what people thought about her? If she'd only been true to herself...but she was in such emotional turmoil at the moment that she felt as if she didn't know who she really was any more.

Oh, for the halcyon days before Richard had arrived and disturbed the even keel of her life! But glancing up at him now, taking in the full impact of his profile, the high cheekbones, the firm chin, the disturbingly sensual mouth, she couldn't help feeling happy that he was there beside her.

They were climbing the wide stone steps that led to the magnificent columns supporting the roof of the terrace. Since the mills of the town had stopped belching out smoke, the stonework had been cleaned and was now the pristine colour of sandstone. It was an imposing building. She remembered having been slightly overawed by it as she'd waited on these very steps all those years ago.

'As a matter of interest, how long is it since you came to a concert here?' Richard asked quietly.

She swallowed hard. 'I haven't been here since I was eighteen. I didn't want to come again after that experience.'

He looked down at her, a puzzled expression in his

eyes. 'Why? What happened here when you were eighteen?'

They were on the terrace now, hemmed in by people on all sides of them. It was like being in the middle of a fast-flowing river.

'Remind me to jog your memory later,' she said quietly.

Once they were installed in their seats near the front of the hall, she felt she could relax. Her cream silk didn't seem so outrageous after all.

She turned to Richard, admiring the superb cut of his charcoal grey suit.

'Lucy was right about the well-dressed dignitaries,' she whispered, as the mayoress swept past, the clinking of her jewellery drowned out by the clanking of the mayoral chain. 'I'm blending in nicely. I wish I'd worn my diamond tiara.'

Richard grinned and took hold of her hand. 'Shall I go back and get it for you?'

The conductor was coming on to the stage.

'Too late!' she whispered, revelling in the feeling of his fingers enclosing hers.

Too soon he removed them, but the glow they'd engendered stayed with her for the whole of the concert. As she listened to the final movement of Beethoven's choral symphony, she felt emotionally moved. This particular section of the symphony always brought tears to her eyes. Impulsively, she leaned across the side of the seat and took hold of Richard's hand.

It was only as he squeezed her fingers that she realised what she'd done. But he was now holding her hand so tightly in his that she couldn't withdraw it. She looked up at him and he smiled the most heart-rending smile.

She smiled back, wiping the tears from her eyes with her other hand.

And at that moment she couldn't differentiate between the ethereal musical experience and the romantic feelings that were churning away inside her, willing her to give in. She turned back to look at the stage, trying to give the impression that she was concentrating on the orchestra and choir.

For Richard, watching Jane as she appeared to be concentrating on the music, the experience was a revelation. He felt as if he was at last beginning to peel off the layers surrounding this complex character. Outwardly so strong and tough, inside she was soft and gentle.

The hand enclosed in his was smaller than he'd realised when he'd first seen her efficiently dealing with her patients. The skin was smooth and sensually exciting to the touch. As he looked at her now, he admired the radiance that shone through her somewhat plain features. She seemed beautiful in an ethereal kind of way.

He could feel desire stirring inside him. He longed to take her in his arms and hold her against him, caressing her gently until he felt the response he hoped he could kindle.

As the clapping started at the end of the concert he released her hand. Jane appeared not to notice as she joined in with the rapturous applause.

He stood up and held out his hand towards her. 'I've booked a table at Giovanni's.'

She smiled. 'Great! I love Italian food. How did you guess?'

'A little bird told me.'

'Mrs Bairstow! That accounts for the fact that everybody knew where we were going tonight!'

'Do you mind?'

'Not if you don't.'

They were pushing through the crowds trying to reach the outer doors.

'Why should I mind?' he asked, a surprised expression on his face.

She didn't reply. Surely he must know what she meant. She remembered all the glamorous girls he'd taken out at medical school whilst she'd been forced to watch enviously from afar.

He suggested it would be better to leave the car in the car park and walk round to the restaurant. As he pushed open the door, Jane could smell the aroma of herbs and spices that she associated with Italian cooking.

'Mmm, I love that smell!'

Richard smiled. Jane had a kind of naïve quality that was distinctly appealing to him. It was one of the things that had first attracted him to Rachel. He pulled himself up sharply as he remembered how he'd vowed never to compare anyone with Rachel. Even after all these years the memories were too poignant for him to bear. But during the last month they'd become a little more bearable. He felt something akin to a guilty pang as he realised the memories were receding.

They started their meal with pasta.

'I always think pasta sets the scene for a successful Italian meal,' Jane said with a huge smile of satisfaction as she rolled up fettuccine with her fork.

'Quite the expert, if I may say so,' Richard said, as he watched her scooping up the pasta. 'I can see you've been here before.'

'Not to this restaurant. It's fiendishly expensive. No, I learned to cope with pasta when I was an impoverished student. There used to be a cheap place in the middle of the shopping precinct.'

She put down her fork. Having referred to her time as a medical student, wouldn't this be the ideal time to challenge him about…?

'I know the place you mean,' he said, temporarily thwarting her intentions. 'I think it was called Antonio's. I used to take all my girlfriends there because it was cheaper than anywhere else.'

She took a deep breath. 'You didn't take me.'

He looked up from his plate, curious to know why she'd adopted that strange tone.

'Well, I didn't know you, did I?'

Her heart was beating so loudly she was glad there was a lot of background noise. But inside her head it was as if the room was in silence.

'Didn't you? Are you sure?'

He reached across the table and took hold of her hand. She snatched it away as if she'd been stung.

'Jane, what is this? What are you getting at?'

It was now or never! 'When I was eighteen, you arranged a date with me,' she said in a flat voice.

'I did what?'

She ignored him. 'You asked me to meet you on the steps of the town hall at seven to go to a concert that started at seven-thirty.'

'My God, you've got a good memory, but I swear I've got absolutely no recollection of—'

'That's because you didn't have to wait outside in the pouring rain, in the middle of winter, shivering and cold and hopelessly humiliated. I waited for over an hour until I realised you weren't going to turn up.'

'Jane, I assure you—'

Richard broke off as the waiter removed the pasta plates. Dear God, had he been so insensitive in his student days that he'd upset one of the younger students? If only he could remember what had really happened. But the fog surrounding the days before Rachel simply wouldn't clear.

'Jane, there were a lot of girls around when I was a medic and—' he began as soon as the waiter had departed.

'I know you were surrounded by adoring females,' she put in harshly, 'but that didn't give you the right to adopt a cavalier attitude to an arrangement. How do you think I felt?'

The waiter was putting down plates of chicken in a wine sauce. Richard could feel his appetite receding as he faced his irate companion.

'I can't begin to imagine how you felt,' he said carefully. 'And if it really was my fault—'

'*If* it was your fault?' Jane repeated angrily, before lowering her voice as she saw the curious glances the people at the next table were giving her. 'Who else could possibly be to blame?'

'But why didn't you say something to me?' he said, his eyes pleading for forgiveness. 'Why didn't you come up to me at medical school and—?'

'You mean, approach the final-year heartthrob? Me, a small fry from the first year? I must say I was surprised you asked me out in the first place.'

She picked up her fork and toyed unsuccessfully with a piece of chicken. It didn't look as if her outburst had done much for Richard's appetite either.

'Look, I didn't mean to spoil our meal,' she said quietly. 'I'd simply meant to jog your memory so that you would perhaps remember why you didn't turn up. I'd hoped you would have said you'd been called to do some last-minute clinical research or you'd been asked to help out in Accident and Emergency or something that would have made me feel I wasn't quite so worthless.'

Having tried unsuccessfully to take hold of her hand, which was now clasped firmly in her lap, he stood up and came round the table. Looking into her eyes, he leaned forward and took her face in his hands.

'Believe me, I would never have done anything to hurt you,' he said quietly. 'When I look back on my student days now it's a complete haze. I feel as if it all happened to someone else. I'm sorry a million times over for hurting you.'

Jane could feel a lump rising in her throat as she looked up into those honest blue eyes. She could see why he might have no recollection of the incident that had caused her first jaundiced view of the opposite sex. Whatever it was that had made him forget their date, she had to forgive him and move on. The younger Rick Montgomery had held a reputation as being a love-'em-and-leave-'em man. She'd never been able to test out the theory. She'd never got beyond first base.

But the present day Richard was a warm-hearted man she couldn't help but admire in every way. She'd never felt like this about anyone and if she continued to harbour an old grudge it would ruin everything.

'I forgive you,' she said quietly.

Slowly he caressed her cheeks. 'Thank you,' he said, his voice husky with emotion as he leaned forward and kissed her on the lips.

She tried to restrain the gasp that threatened to escape her as he straightened himself to his full height and returned to his seat. It was only then she became aware of the curious glances directed their way. She looked across the table but took comfort in the tender expression in Richard's eyes.

'I think this calls for champagne,' he said, raising his hand to attract the attention of one of the waiters. 'Call it the laying of the ghost, because I can see it's been preying on your mind.'

Jane smiled. 'You could say that.'

'And it's over now? I'm one hundred per cent in the clear, am I?' He put his head on one side and pleaded, boyishly, for her approval.

'Ninety-nine per cent,' she conceded. 'But I won't hold it against you.'

'Was that why you were so offhand with me when I first arrived?'

The waiter was unwrapping the foil from the top of the champagne bottle. They both waited for the popping of the cork.

'Partly,' she said carefully. 'But there were other reasons why I didn't welcome having a man about the place.'

'Such as?' He held his foaming glass across the table and clinked it against hers.

She hesitated before taking a sip and then a long drink which made her feel light-headed. 'Hey, if we're both drinking, who's going to drive the monster back to Highdale?'

'I've already thought of that. I'll call a cab and we can come back and collect my car tomorrow.'

She raised an eyebrow. 'We? Did we make a joint decision?'

He grinned. 'Please, Dr Senior Partner, will you give me a lift into Moortown tomorrow after surgery so that I can—?'

Jane laughed. 'Is that how you see me?'

He pulled a wry face. 'Well, you do seem intent on keeping up the image, keeping the upper hand. I don't mind because I think it's only an act put on for my benefit. Anyway, you haven't answered my question. What other reason do you have for distrusting men?'

She was drinking too quickly but feeling less inhibited than she'd ever felt in front of Richard. She put down her glass. 'I've had a series of disastrous romances over the years,' she said slowly.

'Over the years?' he repeated. 'You're only thirty. You make it sound as if you'd reached the end of the line.'

'Funny you should say that,' she said wryly. 'When the most recent man walked out of my life I decided to call a halt to any more romantic ventures.'

'I felt like that when I lost my wife,' he said quietly. 'It was a long time ago.'

'Couldn't have been all that long. You're only—what? Thirty-five?'

He nodded. 'It was a whole lifetime ago, believe me. I'm not the same person I was then.'

The background chatter seemed to break over Jane like waves on a shore, but she chose to ignore it as she watched the agonised expression in Richard's eyes.

'Did she…?'

'Rachel died when she was twenty-seven. We'd been married six months.'

Her heart felt as if it would bleed for him as she listened to his flat tone. 'That certainly puts my own experiences into perspective, Richard,' Jane said softly. 'How long does it take to get over something like that?'

His eyes moistened. 'That's a question I keep asking myself.' He took a deep breath. 'Look, I don't want to spoil the evening by dwelling on the past.'

She reached across to cover his fingers with her own. 'But I want to know more about you.'

He enclosed both her hands in his. 'And I want to

know more about you, but let's talk about the past some other time. I think this evening was the first time I really started looking forward to the future.'

She swallowed hard. 'Me, too.'

What was she saying? She wasn't committing herself to another relationship, was she? Jane pulled herself up sharply. As far as Richard was concerned, chance would be a fine thing! She'd read too much into his words. Coming out this evening with her had simply been an enjoyable experience for him which had helped to blot out the memories of a marriage that had ended all too soon.

She was glad she'd resolved her grudge against him. The last thing she wanted to do was to cause him any more grief. Now that she knew his circumstances she would make a determined effort to be kind.

Being kind would be no effort at all. Preventing herself from going overboard for him would be the problem!

She toyed with the delicious ice cream she'd greedily ordered, feeling the tightening of her waistband. According to the latest dietary statistics, beyond the age of thirty the basal metabolic rate decreased so that the average female put on weight if she didn't reduce her calorie intake. With all her other defects, getting fat would be the last straw!

'Maybe I'll have to go on a diet tomorrow,' she told Richard.

He smiled. 'You don't need to. A few extra pounds would suit you.'

She was relieved to see that he'd recovered his composure. 'Do you really think so? Some people have told me I look scraggy, but after tonight...'

'Slender is the word, not scraggy. You're wonderfully tall and slim.'

'But I'll never look as good as Caroline.'

'Good looks are only skin deep. It's the sum total of a character that adds up to real beauty.'

Jane stared at him. Now, what did he mean by that? The tender expression in his eyes unnerved her. No one had ever paid her compliments about her appearance before. She'd been used to being praised for her brains when she was younger but that was just something she'd inherited. Richard was actually looking at her as if he admired her as a woman.

But she felt that his admiring gaze was, at the same time, critical. How many beautiful women must he have sat opposite on a dinner date? And here she was, in an outdated suit that she'd chosen at the last minute from the depths of her chaotic wardrobe!

You've got to make more effort, she told herself sharply, or he'll lose interest in you.

He was reaching across to pour the last of the champagne into her glass. Had they really drunk the whole bottle? No wonder she felt so deliciously squiffy!

'I'll call a cab,' Richard said, reaching for his mobile. 'We'll have coffee back at my place.'

She smiled across the table at him. Now, that was what she liked. A man who knew his own mind. He knew they both wanted to escape this place and be alone together.

In the back of the cab Jane snuggled against him and he put his arm around her. It all seemed so natural, as if they'd known each other for years. Well, in a way, they had because she'd often thought about him. The magic of the evening had brought back the deep emotional feelings she'd experienced as a young medical student for this handsome, sexy, intensely desirable man. In those days she'd watched him from afar, as it were, longing for him to notice her. But now the unbelievable had happened! She was here with him, his virile body was, oh, so close to hers, his arm was around her, his fingers tantalisingly touching her shoulders.

Jane closed her eyes to savour the bliss of the moment, knowing that she wanted the evening to last for ever. She was well aware that in her uninhibited, champagne-induced state she wanted Richard to make love to her. The present was all that mattered. She would deal with tomorrow and the cold light of reality when it came...

Lying back on the pillows in the half-light of dawn, Jane tried desperately to remember why she was here, in the tiny bedroom above the old stables. She felt fantastic! It was as if she'd shed her old skin and was a completely new creature.

She turned to look at the slumbering figure beside her. In sleep, Richard looked even more desirable than when he was awake. She reached out to touch him, smoothing her fingers over his skin to rekindle some of the sensual feelings she'd experienced the previous night.

He opened his eyes and gave her a long, slow, lazy smile, as if to say that he was unwilling to embrace the day just yet. They were still floating on cloud nine and he had no intention of letting her come down to earth.

Slowly, he reached out for her, gathering her into his arms. Jane made no attempt to stifle the moan that escaped her lips. Her skin, still tingling from their last bout of love-making, sprang to life again and she felt as if her whole body were on fire. As he caressed her with deft strokes of his sensitive fingers she felt the ecstatic sensations mounting once more inside her. She took his face in her hands and placed her lips against his.

Moulding herself against him, she gave herself up to the crescendo of sensations that were claiming her.

Richard teased her with his hands and with his tongue until she felt she couldn't hold the tension any longer. When he entered her, she let out a sigh of pure ecstasy. Slowly her body took up the rhythm of his until they moved as one in their out-of-this-world experience.

She cried out as the ultimate climax claimed her, clinging to him as if she would never let him go. And afterwards, as they lay sated, arms entwined around each other, she felt as if she'd been newly born. She'd never felt like this before...

It was the house martins that awoke her for the second time, and her first thought was of her sister who would be trying to quieten her early-waking son. She looked at the sun rising over the window-sill. Had they really made love without closing the curtains? What if her father had wandered across the courtyard?

Jane pulled the duvet up around her chin. Her father might yet decide to wander out in the early morning. Or Mrs Bairstow might decide to come out looking for Miriam, to call her in for a saucer of milk and some breakfast.

'Isn't it awful, coming back to earth?' she whispered to the other side of the bed.

No reply.

'Richard?' She investigated the mound of duvet.

The door opened and the mystery was solved. Richard came in, wearing a towelling robe. She thought how delightfully dishevelled he looked in a boyish sort of way, his brown hair tumbling over his forehead.

'I've brought coffee to help sober us up.'

She was terribly aware of her nakedness as she took the steaming mug he handed to her. It was one thing to be totally uninhibited during the night when the champagne had removed all inhibitions, but now, in the cold light of day, she would have to pull herself together and come down to earth.

Jane surveyed the crumpled bed. And at that precise moment she realised what she'd done. She'd broken all her resolutions! To say she'd gone overboard was an understatement. How could she ever get back the image she'd tried to maintain since Richard had arrived?

But did she really want to? Wasn't it infinitely more exciting to experience a night like she'd just been through than hang onto some stuffy image? But she'd been here before, hadn't she? Giving in to her natural instincts was the way to get her heart broken.

She groaned. Would she ever learn?

Richard took the mug from her hands and kissed her, oh, so gently on the lips.

'Thank you for last night,' he said huskily. 'If you're feeling less than one hundred per cent this morning, then may I suggest that, from a purely medical point of view, you take the day off. Call it doctor's orders.'

She looked at him, cold reason claiming her back from her idyllic state of never-never land.

'I never take a day off.'

He raised one eyebrow. 'Then maybe you should start now. You're far too efficient. Chill out a bit today. Take the morning off and then we'll go for a walk this afternoon.'

'You know I can't. I've got far too much to do today. Patients to see, house calls to make…'

She was looking around desperately for her clothes. They were scattered across the carpet where they'd been hastily discarded in the frantic desire to reach the bed.

'OK, if you want to play the martyr.'

'I am not playing the martyr! I'm simply trying to be practical.'

As soon as she'd spoken she knew she'd dispelled the magic aura that had still lingered around them.

'I can see that,' Richard said quietly. 'I'll go for a walk until you've got yourself sorted.'

She lay back against the pillows until she heard him pounding down the stone stairs. Running to the window, she watched him crossing the courtyard as he made for the wide wooden gate that led to the path across the fields. He'd hastily pulled on a navy blue fisherman's sweater and a pair of old jeans. She longed, with all her heart, to chase after him, to take hold of his hand, lean close against him and tell the day to take care of itself. She really wanted to play truant!

Jane could see that there was a heavy dew on the grass and a hazy mist was rising up from the valley, shrouding Highdale village completely. Only the tall church spire, emerging from the fluffy camouflage, was caught in the early morning rays of the spring sunshine.

A walk across the fields would be the perfect start to the day. She watched Richard striding out, head held high, in defiant mood. And who could blame him? She'd pricked the bubble, ruined their idyll.

Let's face it, she told herself sharply. I've returned to type. I enjoyed playing the carefree girl last night but it's impossible for me to stay like that.

Her heart was telling her to run after Richard and go with the flow of emotions that had claimed her for the past few hours. But her head was insisting she resume her real self and return to the reality of everyday living.

CHAPTER FOUR

'I'VE got a patient who particularly wants to see you, Jane.'

Jane had already started the engine of her little grey Ford. She didn't realise she was frowning as she wound down the window so she could hear what Richard was saying. She was already later than usual in setting out for her house calls.

Richard leaned on the ledge of her window. 'Don't look so fierce. My guess is it's some kind of gynaecological problem and she's shy in front of a male doctor. She wouldn't even tell me the problem when I offered to bring in Lucy as chaperone. I know I'm upsetting your sacred routine but...'

She put up her hand as she heard the sarcasm creeping into his tone. 'It's OK. There's no need to get personal.'

Jane looked up into the blue eyes that were far too close for comfort, and felt herself melting. She tried to counteract the effect he was having on her by taking a deep breath.

Ever since that idyllic night together, four weeks ago, she'd been unsure how to handle their relationship. Part of her wanted to move along and commit herself to an affair that would last until Richard called a halt. But she knew from painful experience that going down that road would cause her so much unhappiness in the end that she didn't think she could take it again. In fact, she knew she couldn't!

But looking up at him now, she longed to tell him that

she was sorry she'd been so unromantic at the end of their wonderful night. She was sorry she'd poured cold water over everything and called a halt to a wonderful affair before it had started.

Maybe he'd been relieved that she'd appeared not to want to deepen the emotional level of their relationship. Perhaps he'd found someone else to amuse him during his off-duty time or else he'd simply reverted to mourning his wife. Or maybe she'd simply scared him away. Caroline had told her she had that effect on men and she ought to lighten up a bit.

Whatever the reason, they'd had a completely professional relationship since that wonderful evening, and it didn't look as if the experience would ever be repeated.

His expression was purely professional now. She forced herself to concentrate.

'Who's the patient, Richard?'

'Sara Holdsworth.'

'Oh, Sara. I was at primary school in Highdale with her.'

He smiled. 'I thought she'd be a friend of yours. Most of the patients are.'

'OK, I'll go back inside and see her.'

'Do you want me to start on the house calls?' He was opening her car door.

'No, I prefer to do this list. I particularly want to see how Alan Greenwood's getting on since he started taking beta interferon, and I want to check on the state of his living quarters.'

Richard raised one eyebrow and looked down at her. 'And I couldn't do that? What would we all do without you?'

She bridled. 'Now, that's not fair! I can't help taking my work seriously.'

He put one finger under her chin and tilted her face up towards him. It was the first time he'd touched her since that memorable night together and she had to stifle a shiver of desire.

'It suits you, being super-efficient I mean,' he said quietly. 'But sometimes you ought to take a little time off. What have you got planned for this afternoon?'

Her heart started beating madly. 'It's clear unless we get an emergency.'

'Why don't I ring the deputising service and tell them we need cover for the afternoon? A walk over the fells would be marvellous on a day like this.'

The bleating of a lamb over in the field seemed to second this remark. Jane hesitated. Wasn't this what she'd secretly hoped for during the last four weeks? Taking up where they'd left off?

'Sounds like a good idea,' she said carefully. 'But we'll have to be back for the evening surgery.'

His expression became very solemn. 'I wouldn't dream of disrupting the smooth flow of the practice.'

'Right! I'll go and see Sara,' she said briskly.

He followed her inside, close behind her until they separated and went into their own consulting rooms.

Sara's face lit up as Jane went in. 'Thanks for coming back, Jane. I was afraid I'd missed you. Dr Montgomery has a lovely, sympathetic manner but I felt I could talk to you better. I've started putting weight on round my tummy and I haven't had a period for nearly five months.'

Jane smiled. 'Well, that seems like an easy diagnosis to me.'

She ran her eyes over Sara's ample figure. She'd always been a plump girl and she remembered how some of the children had teased her when they'd been at school. She'd put on a lot of weight since childhood and so a five-month pregnancy could remain undetected, hidden beneath the extra folds of flesh.

'Sara, if I could test a sample of your urine I could—'

'I did test it, this morning. I bought one of those pregnancy kits from the chemist. And it came out positive. But I can't be pregnant!'

Jane saw the anguished look in her patient's eyes. This wasn't going to be easy.

'What makes you think you can't be pregnant, Sara?' she asked gently.

'Because I've been taking the Pill every day. I wouldn't dare miss one. Ray would be furious if I did.'

'So Ray doesn't want you to get pregnant?'

'Absolutely not! He made me agree we should wait until we've got more money coming into the house before we start a family.'

'And how do you feel about it?'

Sara shifted uneasily on the chair. 'Well, I wanted to start a family as soon as we were married. I mean, I'm thirty already and I think it's good to be young with your children. But I can see Ray's point. It's a lot easier bringing up children if you can afford to feed and clothe them properly.'

'Have you been taking any other medicines while you've been taking the Pill, Sara?'

'Nothing at all!' Sara paused as if racking her brains. 'Apart from a harmless herbal remedy my mother bought for me at the chemist. I was going through a bad patch with my nerves—nothing serious or I would have come to see you. Just feeling a bit under the weather and depressed. I think it was partly to do with the fact that Ray and I kept rowing about when we were going to start a family.'

Jane leaned back in her chair. 'This herbal remedy—what's it called?'

'St John's wort. My mother swears by it as a pick-me-up.'

'Ah!' Everything fell into place. Jane was remembering an article she'd read in her medical journal some time ago. 'Some research has been done into the effect of St John's wort when it's taken in conjunction with other medication. It has an adverse effect on several drugs, one of which is the oral contraceptive. It can increase the risk of pregnancy.'

'My God! So you really think I am pregnant?'

Jane hesitated. In her own mind she had no doubt about it. 'If you'd like to get up on the examination couch, I'll let you know.'

She ran her fingers over Sara's abdomen before putting on sterile gloves so that she could do an internal examination.

'You've got a healthy baby in there, Sara. Would you like to listen to your baby's heartbeat?'

She was holding the foetal stethoscope, a trumpet-shaped instrument, directly over Sara's womb.

As if in a dream, Sara leaned forward and placed her ear to the stethoscope. A look of complete incredulity passed over her face.

'So it's true! I can't believe it. Oh, the dear little thing… But what am I going to tell Ray? I daren't!'

Jane took hold of her hand. 'You'll have to, Sara,' she said quietly. 'It's too late to do a termination.'

Sara frowned. 'Oh, I could never do that! I want this baby, but Ray doesn't.'

'I've met this situation with other patients,' Jane said carefully. 'And in every case the father has ended up being besotted by the unexpected baby.'

'Will you come round and talk to Ray?' Sara said in a pleading voice. 'I need some moral support when I tell him.'

'You ought to tell him as soon as you can.'

'He's on the early shift at the factory in Moortown. He'll be home this afternoon if you could make it.'

'Don't worry, I'll be there.'

So much for the walk over the fells with Richard!

'Do you think Dr Montgomery would come with you? If there was another man there, Ray wouldn't dare get as angry as he sometimes does.'

'I'll see what I can do.'

Perhaps they could combine their mission of mercy with a walk. She would see what Richard thought of the idea.

Driving down to the village with the top of Richard's car down, Jane was feeling apprehensive about the outcome of the confrontation with Sara's husband.

'Sara's husband, Ray, is a difficult character,' she told Richard. 'He was also at primary school with us and I remember he was always starting fights in the school playground. I'm glad you've come with me.'

Briefly, he glanced sideways. 'He's not physically violent now, is he?'

'Not that I know of, but Sara certainly seems scared of him. It's such a pity because she's obviously thrilled at the prospect of a baby.'

'She'd been taking St John's wort, you said? The chemists will have to start warning their customers to check if their herbal remedies have adverse effects on their prescribed medicines. Most pharmacists do, but this is fairly recent research and the findings of the report haven't reached all of the medical fraternity.'

She leaned back against the seat, pulling the knot in her scarf tight under her chin as she wished she'd had time to wash her dishevelled hair that morning. She was getting a bit fed up with it. Since Richard had arrived she'd been conscious of her hair every day. It didn't just have to look good on special occasions. Every day was becoming a special occasion for her!

Maybe she should splash out on one of those expensive hairstyles in Leeds? The last time she'd been to the salon over there she'd been trying to impress Paul. That was what was holding her back now. The thought that she was committing herself again. Would she be in danger of losing her own identity if she gave in to a bit of luxurious pampering? Wasn't trying to please a man the first step towards becoming his emotional slave?

'You're very quiet,' he said gently. 'Don't worry. I've dealt with patients' irate husbands before.'

She felt guilty that she'd allowed her thoughts to wander away from their difficult assignment.

'I'm not worrying,' Jane said quickly. 'Sara's husband is quite a small man. We're both bigger than he is.'

Richard smiled. 'I hope we won't have to resort to brute force.'

He parked the car outside the small terrace house at the side of the main street in Highdale. Jane noticed the freshly painted windows and doors and the brightly shining brass knocker that Richard was now grasping.

The door opened almost immediately.

'Thanks for coming,' Sara said, in a quiet voice. 'Ray's watching sport on television in the front room. Come through.'

Jane took a deep breath as she followed her patient down the narrow hallway.

'Not a good time to break the news, when a man is watching sport,' Richard whispered.

Jane nodded. 'That's what I was thinking. But we've got to do it.'

Ray looked up when the two doctors walked into his sitting room. 'What's all this about?'

He glanced up at his wife who had picked up the remote and turned off the sound on the television.

Not a good move! Jane thought apprehensively. 'Hello, Ray. This is my new partner at the surgery, Dr Richard Montgomery. We've come to have a chat with you and Sara. May we sit down?'

Sara waved a hand towards the sofa.

'Can I get you a cup of tea or—?' she began, but her husband cut her short.

'Stop fussing, woman! Let's hear what the doctors have to say first.'

Jane looked across at Richard, wondering where she should start.

Richard cleared his throat. 'Mr Holdsworth, this may come as a surprise. Sara has been taking a herbal remedy that cancelled out the effect of her contraceptive Pill. She—'

'You stupid woman!' Ray was on his feet. 'It's that stuff your dozy mother gave you, isn't it? Well, you know what you can do, don't you? We can't afford a baby and that's final!'

Sara had begun to cry. Jane stood up and put her arm round her shoulders.

'Ray, you're going to have to face up to this,' she said firmly. 'It's no good playing the big bully when you've got a wife and child to think about. This baby isn't going to go away, so the sooner you accept it, the better.'

For a moment, Jane thought the erstwhile playground

bully was going to put his fists up against her. She knew she'd been pushing her luck but it was the only language he understood.

Ray's lip curled. 'Anybody can see why you never got married, Jane Crowther! No man in his right mind would take on a bossy woman like you! I've always been the boss in my own home and that's the way it's going to stay. You needn't think you can walk in here and—'

'Now, just a minute,' Richard said, sternly. 'Dr Crowther is simply doing her job. Sara is her patient and we're both very concerned for her welfare. If you love your wife you'll have to give her some consideration. This is a very difficult time for her.'

He moved across the little room and sat down on the sofa beside the irate husband.

'Now, tell me, Ray, tell me why you really don't want this baby?' he said, in a professional but soothing voice.

'Because we agreed not to have one yet and Sara shouldn't have got herself pregnant,' he replied petulantly.

'With the greatest respect,' Richard said, 'Sara didn't get pregnant by herself.'

Ray scowled. 'But we can't afford a baby!'

'I've got that money in my savings account,' Sara said nervously.

Her husband ran a hand over his thinning hair. 'That's for the new carpet. You said yourself you were tired of making do with all the shabby old stuff your mum threw out.'

'Well, it doesn't seem important now. We don't need anything new, Ray,' Sara said gently. 'Just a new baby.'

Richard stood up so that Sara could sink down on the sofa beside her husband. She had put out a tentative hand towards him, her eyes pleading with him to accept the situation.

'I was saving up to buy a car,' he mumbled. 'What happens if you start having the baby and I've no car to take you to the hospital. I can't go taking you on the bus!'

'Oh, Ray!' Sara grabbed hold of her husband's hand. 'You'll love having a baby! We'll be a proper family.'

'Think how happy you'll make the grandparents,' Jane said quickly, sensing the tide was turning. 'Sara's parents will be over the moon and they'll help you out.'

Ray pulled a wry face. 'My own mum will stop nagging me, that's for sure. Always on about when she's going to be a grandma.' He paused, and looked around. 'OK, I suppose I've no choice really. If it's on its way, that's it, isn't it?'

He put his arm round his wife's ample shoulders. She snuggled against him.

'I'm not getting up to feed it in the night!' Ray said firmly.

Sara smiled dreamily. 'You won't need to. I'll do everything...'

Jane smiled at Richard. 'I think we should be moving off now. Come and see me in the surgery, Sara, and I'll fix up your antenatal care at the hospital.'

'Phew! That could have been tricky!' Jane leaned back against the passenger seat as Richard accelerated out of the village. 'What on earth Sara ever saw in Ray I'll never know!'

Richard took his hand off the steering-wheel and took hold of hers. 'Love does strange things to people,' he said quietly. 'Haven't you ever fallen in love with an unlikely character?'

'I've been out with some unsuitable men, that's for sure,' she replied. 'Paul was my worst mistake but, with the benefit of hindsight, I'm not so sure I was ever in love with him.'

'Tell me about him.'

'No! Well, not now, anyway,' she added in a placatory tone. 'I don't want to spoil a beautiful afternoon like this.'

They'd reached the top of the hill that looked down into the Highdale valley. Far below, she could see the ribbon of shining water, where she'd learned to swim as a child, snaking its way between the trees.

'It's so good to get away,' Jane said, half to herself.

'We should get away more often,' he told her, his voice gentle.

Oh, yes, they should! Being alone with Richard up here among her beloved fells, it was her idea of bliss. She was thinking no further than the afternoon. The future could take care of itself.

Richard parked the car at the top of a rough track and they scrambled down to a small stream. Gently, he pulled her down beside him, leaning against the warm surface of a large, smooth boulder. It seemed perfectly natural that she should snuggle against him as he put his arm around her.

The feel of his hard muscular body against her was setting her pulses racing. She wasn't going to hold back if they moved on a step. But Richard seemed to be playing it cool. Perhaps he felt they'd jumped too far ahead last time. They were, after all, relative strangers.

'I wish I knew more about you, Richard,' she said quietly. 'I mean apart from what you wrote on your CV about educational qualifications and all that stuff. I didn't even know you'd been married when you first arrived.'

He drew in his breath. 'It's not something I discuss…with everybody.'

'Were you very much in love with…?'

'With Rachel? Yes. We were very happy together. I'd had loads of girlfriends but she was the first one who was interested in my mind as well as my body.'

He broke off and gave a rueful grin. 'That sounds very highfallutin but you know what it was like when we were medical students. Bed-hopping was a natural sport but finding someone with the same interests was more difficult.'

Jane felt a pain deep down inside her. How could she ever compete with a paragon like Rachel?

'You obviously adored her,' she said softly, shifting her position so that she wasn't quite so close. It was difficult to talk about another woman while you were experiencing sensual waves of feeling from contact with the man who had loved her.

'It didn't last long enough,' he said quietly. 'We met when I was a junior registrar at St Celine's in London. Rachel had spent a year as a house surgeon and was then training at the Hospital for Tropical Diseases. We got married as soon as she'd finished the course and then we applied for a couple of posts on the medical staff of a hospital in Bangkok.'

She heard the catch in his voice and her heart went out to him. Moving closer again, she looked up into his expressive eyes. But he was staring into space, reliving the memories.

'Was Bangkok where…?'

'I was in Bangkok when I heard that Rachel had died,' he said flatly. 'She'd gone upcountry for a week to visit a remote hill tribe, who had become prone to an unknown disease. I had wanted to go with her but the hospital insisted I continue with my surgical work. I had a heavy schedule that week.' He broke off.

Jane waited silently, aware that he mightn't continue but unwilling to prompt him until he was ready.

'Apparently, there was a violent storm. Rachel was crossing a clearing in the trees to go into a village house where there was a sick child. There was a sudden streak of lightning. She took the full blast and...died instantly.'

Jane shivered. It was too awful to contemplate. No wonder Richard's eyes were moist with tears.

He was pulling himself to his feet. 'Come on, let's walk. I didn't want to depress you.'

She took hold of the hand he was holding out towards her. 'I'm glad you told me. I'd no idea what you must have been through. How on earth did you start to come to terms with it?'

There was a haunted expression in his eyes as he looked down at her. 'You told me your father went to pieces after your mother died. I was exactly the same. I didn't see any point in living any more. I resigned from the hospital and for a while I simply drifted around Thailand, sleeping rough. I had a few belongings in a rucksack. Sometimes I paid a small sum of money and rented a little shack on the beach. I made no plans for the future. I just existed. Looking back, I consider that period of my life to be my lost years.'

Richard began to quicken his pace. The path was now too narrow to walk side by side so she fell into step behind him.

'How long did you stay like that?'

He turned round and put his hands on her shoulders. She was glad she could stop walking because she was becoming breathless, trying to keep up the pace he'd set. It was as if he was trying to escape from the past.

'I was in this state of limbo for about two years,' he said quietly.

'And then, one day, I was swimming out to sea and I had the urge to keep swimming, to blot it all out, maybe to end it all. And it was at that point that I knew I'd reached rock bottom. There was nothing beyond but oblivion or clawing my way back to reality. I remember there was a dolphin swimming close beside me. It was frisking up into the air, looking so happy. And I told myself that eventually I would be happy again but…' His voice broke off. When he spoke his voice was hardly audible. 'I just didn't realise how long it would take.'

'Sometimes time is the only real healer,' Jane said gently, as she pulled his face down towards her.

There was a look of surprise in his eyes as he bent his head. Her kiss was meant to be one of pure compassion but the touch of his lips excited her so much that she allowed herself to linger longer than she'd meant to. But as she began to pull away he held her closer against him, his arms tightening around her.

His kiss deepened before, very gently, he held her away from him, looking down at her with real tenderness.

'Time alone can't heal,' he said huskily. 'It needs a great deal of help. I think I'm getting the right treatment.'

He took her hand as he began to walk along the streamside path. 'If we walk over this hill we can take the path down into Deepdale,' he told her, his voice sounding brighter.

She was glad he'd told her something about his past but relieved that they were now back in the present day. With the June sunshine lighting up the glorious golden glow of the gorse bushes, she felt her spirits lifting again.

'I do know where Deepdale is,' she said, suddenly re-membering with a slight pang of apprehension that the

Montgomerys lived there. 'Is there any reason why we should go down there?'

He smiled. 'No reason at all, except I thought you might like some home-made scones and a cup of tea.'

She hesitated. 'I think you just talked me into it. But I don't mind telling you I feel a bit scared. I've never met a real live film star before.'

'Oh, but you have! When I was ten my mother agreed to open a fête that your mother had arranged. It was in aid of some charity, I believe, and my mum is a great one for good causes. Anyway, it was the day she was due to drive me back to boarding school, so I had to come with her and hang around your house until we could escape.'

Jane's eyes widened. 'And was I there? I don't remember anything about it.'

He gave her a wry grin. 'I remember you! You were about five and you spent the whole time bossing your little sister around. Admittedly, she was being a real pain, as I recall, and your mother was too busy with the cups of tea... Talking of which, I'm getting decidedly thirsty so let's get a move on.'

She followed him down the steep, sloping path where it was only possible to walk in single file.

The Montgomery farm was spread out over a large area at the side of the river. Walking along the long track from the five-barred gate, Jane was beginning to wish she hadn't agreed to come. She felt decidedly dishevelled in her jeans and T-shirt. Wearing casual clothes for her visit to Sara's and Ray's had been a deliberate ploy to set them at ease, but now, after a couple of hours on the fells, she knew she must look a complete mess!

And from the pictures she'd seen in the newspapers of

Sylvia Montgomery, she expected to feel decidedly overawed.

The smile on Richard's mother's face as she opened
the kitchen door dispelled some of her apprehension.

'Richard! What a lovely surprise! And you've
brought...?'

'Mum, this is Jane from Highdale Practice. We were
out walking and—'

'I thought you must be Jane Crowther. I'm so glad to
meet you again. I met you when you were a child but I
haven't seen you since. Come in and have some tea. Do
you want to freshen up, Jane, as you've been walking
over the fells?'

Did she ever! She disappeared into the downstairs
cloakroom and began to make herself look vaguely pre-
sentable.

She washed her hands then raked a comb through her
hair. It wouldn't stay in place. She dipped the comb in
some cold water. Now it looked wet but no better! A
radical change of hairstyle was necessary and the sooner
the better! It would be worth every penny.

Richard's father Desmond looked like an older brother.
His hair was steely grey but thick, and the high cheek-
boned features were almost identical. A few wrinkles
around the eyes and forehead pronounced that he'd lived
a few years longer, but he had a youthful manner as he
came across the large, quarry tiled kitchen, his hand ex-
tended towards her.

'So you're the clever doctor who held the fort over at
Highdale when your father had to retire. Great to meet
you, Jane!'

He was holding onto her hand with a firm grasp.

'I don't know about being clever. I didn't have a

choice but to keep going. It was a great relief when Richard came to ease the load.'

'It was a great relief when Richard came back to the Dales,' his mother said, pouring hot water into a brown earthenware teapot that she'd placed on the long wooden refectory table. 'We were thrilled when he came back from the Far East and started his GP training in Leeds. I knew there wasn't a vacancy anywhere around this area so when our doctor over at Settle told me about the Highdale vacancy I phoned Richard immediately.'

Richard's father pulled up a chair at the table for Jane. 'It turned out that Richard had already applied, so we knew he was keen.'

'I'm sorry your father had to retire,' Sylvia Montgomery said in her gentle, fascinatingly eloquent voice. 'But I don't think we would have got our son back here if there hadn't been an interesting job to tempt him. We've been begging him to come home ever since he was left on his own out there in the Far East.'

As she'd been speaking she'd set out blue and white china teacups and saucers on the table in front of them. Desmond Montgomery was carrying scones, clotted cream and jam from a side table.

'Come on, help yourself,' Sylvia said, pushing the plate of scones towards Jane before taking one for herself. 'We don't stand on ceremony at this house.'

Jane looked at the arrow-slim figure of Richard's mother, the impeccable long blonde, silky hair and the still beautiful classical features. Sylvia Montgomery had been called the typical English rose in her younger days.

'You haven't changed since the photos I used to see of you in magazines, Sylvia,' she said. 'How on earth do you do it?'

Sylvia smiled as she exchanged a look with her husband. 'With difficulty at the moment. It was easier when I was younger, but now that age is catching up with me I spend a lot of time and money on myself. Always hoping for that elusive part that I haven't been offered in years.'

She gave a wide, beautiful smile that showed off her perfect teeth as she held up her perfectly manicured hands with their long, shiny, crimson nails.

'I've never had to do any rough work. People assume that because I live in a farmhouse I must know all about farming but I don't know one end of a cow from the other. Neither does Desmond. We simply bought this place because it was in such a beautiful part of England and it's fairly commutable. Desmond's law practice is based in Leeds and even when he has to go down to London it's an easy journey.'

'I rent out all the pasture land to a neighbouring farmer,' Desmond said. 'So we get the advantage of being surrounded by fields without any of the work.'

'And before you ask,' Sylvia cut in, 'I didn't make these delicious scones. I have a wonderful, very capable woman who comes in every morning and sorts me out.'

Her husband reached across the table and patted her hands. 'But you're beautiful and talented, my darling.'

Sylvia gave a self-deprecatory tinkling laugh. 'Try telling that to my agent! More tea, Jane?'

Jane pushed her cup nearer to the teapot. 'Yes, please.'

Richard was looking across to the wide casement windows. Something seemed to be bothering him. She took a sip of her tea as she watched him get up from his chair and walk over to the window.

'I don't know what those kids think they're doing, larking about by the river, but somebody ought to warn them about the strong current down there.'

'I've put a sign up by the stile but nobody takes any notice,' Desmond said, getting up from the table to join his son. 'That narrow section between the rocks is almost as dangerous as the Strid over at Bolton Abbey. That's why I never let you swim there as a child. It looks as if that young idiot is going to try and jump across it. We'd better—'

'No!' Richard had turned away from the window and was striding across the kitchen. He glanced at Jane as he passed her. 'There's a young man just gone into the water. I'll go and see what I can do. Dad, phone for an ambulance. Jane, you come with me.'

She was already on her feet, trying desperately to keep up with Richard's long strides. He broke into a run as they left the farmyard and began crossing the field. The screams of terror from the youngsters gathered by the river came wafting up towards her, sending a cold chill down her spine. As she ran behind Richard, she was praying they would get down to the river in time to avert a tragedy.

CHAPTER FIVE

THERE were five youths screaming with terror on the river-bank. One of them had begun stripping off to go into the water to find his friend but the others were holding him back. It was obvious that the brown, swirling water in the narrow stretch between the rocks would have swallowed him up, too. They looked round, and their faces registered relief as Richard and Jane arrived.

Jane found herself treading on empty beer bottles and discarded sandwiches as she hurried to the riverside. The frightened boys couldn't have been more than fourteen or fifteen. Probably bunking off school for an illicit picnic which had gone terribly wrong.

'Sean's gone under,' one of the boys said, his teeth chattering with fear. 'We dared him to jump across to the other side. What can we do?'

'Don't go in after him,' Richard said firmly. 'Your friend fell in at the worst point where the water is like a whirlpool. The current will swirl him around but very shortly it should hopefully carry him downstream and then…there he is! You can follow me and we'll try to reach him in the calmer section of the river.'

The boys, relieved at being able to do something, raced after Richard, Jane bringing up the rear. It was a fast-flowing current and the body that had surfaced in the centre of the river looked pale and lifeless. As she ran she was trying to calculate how long the youth had been submerged. How many minutes had it been since Richard had been standing at the window? It seemed like a life-time.

Further downstream, as Richard had predicted, the dangerous current had eased but the seemingly lifeless body was still floating way out of reach in the middle of the river.

'I'm going to swim out to him,' Richard said tersely, as he pulled off his shoes.

'Be careful!' Jane said, but she knew he was thinking only about saving a life—if there was still a life to be saved.

She shivered as she watched him plunge in, fully clothed. The sun was still high in the late afternoon June sky but she knew the water would be cold. And although the flow of the water was less swift in this section of the river, she could still see that Richard, although a strong swimmer, was having difficulty reaching the young man as he battled against the current.

She held her breath as he grabbed hold of the inert figure and hauled him onto his back, holding him against his chest. Swimming back, with the added burden of a dead weight on top of him, was obviously taxing all Richard's strength. The journey back to the bank seemed endless.

Jane breathed a deep sigh of relief as he reached it. One of the boys was holding out his hand, and Richard took it. Two others took the weight of their friend and hauled him onto the grass. Richard was panting heavily. It was up to her to try and revive the victim while Richard got his breath back.

'Move back, boys,' she said quickly.

There wasn't a moment to be lost. Every second counted in a drowning case. She knelt down on the grass and leaned across the boy as she felt for a pulse. There wasn't one, neither was there any movement from the chest. She turned her patient onto his side and a gush of foam-like froth emptied itself onto the grass.

She placed her hand on the boy's throat and put her fingers in his mouth as she tried to clear an airway. She noticed that his face was congested and livid in colour as she bent down, closed the nostrils by pinching them with her thumb and index finger before sealing her lips over the young patient's mouth and blowing gently into his lungs, two slow full breaths with a pause in between. She found herself willing him to breathe but his body seemed lifeless.

Richard put a hand on her shoulder. 'There's still no pulse. I'll begin chest compressions. We'll work in tandem. Give two breaths, Jane, and I'll follow with fifteen compressions.'

They repeated this sequence four times before checking the boy's pulse again. Still no sign of life. Jane took a deep breath and bent her head over the patient's mouth once more.

As Richard checked for a pulse after several more sequences of treatment, he called out, excitedly. 'There's a faint pulse!'

At the same moment, Jane noticed a slight movement in the young man's chest.

'His chest moved, Richard! He's breathing!'

She began to feel hope rising inside her and relief that Richard hadn't been swept away in that dangerous river. In all the excitement she hadn't had time to contemplate how she would have lived without him if he'd been sucked underneath the surface by the treacherous current.

As they worked together to save a life, Jane knew without a shadow of a doubt that she loved Richard. She'd tried so hard to remain dispassionate but it had just happened against her will. She was completely hooked and there was nothing she could do to fight against it now. She would just have to go along until he tired of her and she was left to pick up the pieces of her broken heart.

There was a slight spluttering sound from the boy. She turned him on his side as more water gushed from his mouth and then, miraculously, his eyes fluttered open and he stared straight at her.

'Who are you?'

She smiled. 'I'm Jane Crowther, Sean. You fell in the river and we had to fish you out.'

The young man groaned. 'I feel awful.'

From lower down the valley Jane could hear the reassuring sound of an ambulance.

'Don't worry, Sean. We're going to take you over to Moortown General and you'll be in safe hands there.'

Jane put down the phone and reached for the case notes she'd written up concerning Sean. He wasn't one of her patients at the practice but since the near tragedy yesterday she'd become heavily involved with the case and had just finished a long discussion with his consultant at the hospital. Richard would be relieved, when he got back from doing the house calls, to hear that Sean was making good progress, although he was still very weak and they were going to keep him in hospital for a few more days.

She looked out of the window, her eyes automatically fixing on the road that Richard would return by. She realised she was losing control of her emotions as she turned into a lovesick teenager! At the age of eighteen she'd mooned over this man and he'd let her down. She'd been heartbroken. He'd now said he was sorry, but could a leopard change his spots?

No! The answer was emphatically no, and the more she went along with these immature feelings, the more she was going to get hurt. She'd managed to forget him over the years…well, not entirely! He'd always been there somewhere in her subconscious as the ultimate she might aspire to. Was it possible that there was only one man in the world who was the perfect partner for her?

But she wasn't the perfect partner for him! She ran a hand through her tangled mass of hair. At least she could make an effort to change her appearance. If they were going to have a memorable affair she didn't want Richard's memories of her to be of someone who couldn't care less about her appearance.

When she considered the women who'd shared his life so far she felt hopelessly out of her depth. First of all there had been his impeccably groomed mother who, no doubt, would have bent over his cot without a hair out of place. Then there had been the hordes of lovely female medics and nurses who'd made it obvious they'd fancied him rotten. And as for the beautiful and talented Rachel…

Decisively, Jane reached for the phone again and di-alled the number of the ultra-chic hairdressing salon in Leeds.

'Oh, you have a cancellation with André this after-noon?' she heard herself saying apprehensively.

She hadn't meant to take the plunge quite so quickly! She'd planned to have a few days in which to muse upon how drastic a change she required. André was their top stylist who'd shaved her head almost down to the scalp when she'd thought she'd been in love with Paul, and he'd charged her a fortune! She'd felt like an escaped convict during the long weeks it had taken to grow back.

'I don't want anything too radical today,' Jane began in a faltering tone.

'André will be able to advise you, madam,' she was told before the line went dead.

As she stood up and went over to the window, she wondered why it was that she found a visit to the hair salon more daunting than taking a medical exam. Was it because she was way out of her depth in the beauty department? Some women, like Sylvia Montgomery, had spent a whole lifetime working on their appearance, whereas she'd only given the occasional grudging few minutes in the middle of her busy life.

But this afternoon she was going to be firm with André! She wanted a transformation but, as she'd told the receptionist on the phone, nothing too radical.

Jane had time to contemplate the impending transformation as she sat in the plush reception area, waiting until her stylist was free. Thumbing through the glossy magazine that was devoted entirely to hairstyles, she felt again the same sense of impending doom that she'd felt last time.

Out of the corner of her eye, she could see that there was some kind of discussion going on between the staff surrounding the reception desk. Glances were being cast in her direction. She tried to bury her shiny face in the magazine. Were they deciding they didn't have a comb strong enough to untangle her mass of hair?

With a sense of relief she heard the receptionist explaining that André had been double booked and would she mind terribly if Michael did her hair? She willingly agreed to the change, especially as Michael, the new stylist, was younger and much less intimidating.

He actually listened to what she was saying, nodding

occasionally and becoming totally involved with her. Taking a lock of Jane's newly shampooed and high-lighted hair, he gently snipped at the ends, softly shaping it around her face. Then he smoothed in some mousse that straightened the frizzy curls into manageable waves.

Delighted with the result, she took two bottles of the magic mousse before paying the astronomical bill. She told herself it was worth every penny as she handed over her credit card. In the mirror above the reception desk she could see that the new style, although shorter, still covered her ears, and the gentle waves over her forehead had a softening effect on her features. She hadn't expected a miracle but this was a pretty good second!

Strolling along Bond Street, Jane couldn't help sneaking a glance at her reflection in the shop windows. Taking a closer look at one of them, she noticed a well-cut, oat-meal-coloured, linen trouser suit. She thought of the cotton skirts and blouses she usually wore now that it was high summer when she went on her house calls. When Richard went with her she felt decidedly frumpy.

The shop assistant thought that madam looked very elegant in the new suit. And wouldn't this little cream silk blouse be perfect underneath? This darling little scarf at the neck perhaps? And what about shoes? Madam's shoes were totally unsuitable. Some new underwear would give her the feel of luxury so necessary with a new outfit, didn't she think?

Jane's credit card took a hefty bashing before she decided she had to call a halt to this impulsive spending spree. She felt exhilarated, so much so that she decided to wear her new ensemble and have the assistant pack away her boring cotton dress, jacket and sandals.

Parking the car in front of the house when she got home, she could see Richard standing by the window of

the sitting room. She was glad he'd been keeping her
father company while she'd been out, but she didn't feel
she could face him just yet in her transformed state. She
took a deep breath, gathered up her parcels and ran up
the stone steps. She planned to hurry up the stairs to her
room and slip into jeans and T-shirt.

The sitting-room door opened as she was creeping
past.

'Jane! Is it really you?'

Richard's grin spread across the whole of his handsome face.

She froze. 'Very funny! You're going to say you didn't
recognise me, aren't you?'

'I thought a stranger had pinched your car when you
got out. What have you done to yourself? You look completely different.'

'That was my intention,' she said defiantly. 'I'm sorry
if you don't like what you see but—'

He moved a step closer. 'Jane, you look lovely!'

'Don't go over the top! Lovely I will never be, but I
thought it was time I smartened myself up.'

He was standing very near to her now. Slowly he
reached out and touched her newly styled hair. 'I like
this! It makes you look sort of...chic.'

Jane threw back her head and laughed. 'Now you really are having me on!'

She looked up into his eyes and revelled in the genuine
admiration she could see mirrored there. He bent towards
her and for one heady moment she thought he was going
to kiss her. But he simply lowered his voice and whispered that her father had called him in because he wasn't
feeling well.

'What's the problem?' she asked anxiously.

'I've checked him out,' he said quietly. 'His blood

pressure's slightly raised but there's been no deterioration in the condition of his heart. His cardiac pacemaker is still controlling the beats. I told him he's been overdoing things in the garden but he insists it wasn't that.'

Jane pulled a wry face. 'It never is! Alf, our part-time gardener, would love to do extra hours, but Dad likes to feel he can still work as hard as he did before his heart attack. You'd think as a doctor he would take more care of himself.'

Richard smiled. 'He subscribes to the theory that cardiac patients should get plenty of exercise, which is absolutely true. But it's the balance between exercise and rest that he's getting wrong.'

'Try telling him that!'

'I just did,' Richard said.

Jane's eyes widened. 'And…?'

'He said he'd bear it in mind.'

'Well, you've had more influence than I ever have!'

Her concern for her father had made her forget that she'd planned to change out of her finery. Dumping her parcels in the hall, she went in to see him.

'Ah, the wanderer returns!' Her father looked up and smiled. 'I could hear you two whispering about me out there in the hall. Are you going to call in the vet and have me put down?'

'Something like that,' Jane said, casting an expert eye over her father.

He was definitely paler than usual, but if Richard had checked him out she wouldn't worry too much. She kissed his cold cheek before sitting down on the sofa beside him, resisting the desire to reach out for his thin wrist and take his pulse. There was nothing she could do that Richard hadn't already done.

Her father was staring at her. 'You look different. Where's all your hair?'

'On the shop floor. I've been to the hairdresser's.'

'Well, at least they haven't chopped it all off this time!'

He glanced across at Richard who was standing by the fireplace and gave him a conspiratorial wink. 'Last time she had a new hairdo it was because she was going out to some fancy dinner-dance at the Moortown Golf Club with that fellow…what was his name? Paul something or other? She'd bought a posh new frock but didn't like her hair so she had it all shaved off.'

Jane stood up and moved over to the window, looking out across the garden. Why did her father have to remind her of her humiliation? He could be so insensitive. He just didn't seem to realise when he was hurting her feelings. He'd always thought she was as tough as she seemed on the outside and she'd been too proud to put him straight.

'It was supposed to be a chic hairstyle but it didn't suit me,' she said in a firm voice.

'I thought it looked terrible,' her father continued relentlessly. 'And I don't think Paul liked it much either because he never came round again.'

He gave his daughter a quizzical look. 'Whatever happened to Paul? I know he sold that damn great house of his and then he just disappeared.'

'He went back to Australia,' she said quietly, terribly aware that Richard was watching her and taking in every word.

Her father clapped his hands together. 'Now I remember! There was an old girlfriend turned up and went to live with him for a while before he left. One of my patients told me.'

Jane strode over to the door. 'I'm going up to change before evening surgery.'

As she closed the door she heard her father asking Richard if he thought she was upset about something. She didn't stay long enough to hear his reply.

The last patient had just gone. It had been a quiet session. There had been no emergencies. Mrs Jenkins had called in, complaining about problems associated with her asthmatic chest, and Jane had given her another lesson in how to use her asthma apparatus. She hadn't quite got the hang of it and Jane had made a note to call in and ask her daughter, who lived next door to her, if she could pop in to see her mother as often as she could.

She'd done a couple of antenatal examinations for young expectant mothers who were still working and found it easier to see Jane than trek into Moortown after work. Sara had called in to thank Jane for helping her win round her husband over the expected baby and Jane had organised the antenatal care for her at the hospital.

Finally, she'd reassured an elderly rheumatism patient that she would call in and see him at home every few weeks when the summer finished.

Looking out of the window at the sun, sinking lower in the evening sky, it was difficult to imagine the harsh winter that would descend on the fells in a few months' time. She loved the summer months. Life seemed so much easier then, both for her and for her patients. In the winter she always worried about the sick and elderly patients in their lonely farms and cottages. But that was the tough life the country folk had been born to and they had strong characters to battle with the elements. A few of her patients had moved to the town when they'd become older, but they'd always told her they missed the fells and the moorland.

A knock on the door roused Jane from her musing. She was surprised when Richard walked in.

'I thought you were off duty this evening,' she said.

'I am, which is why I've come to invite you over for supper. I've been down to Highdale to buy the ingredients, and as I drove back I began wondering who I could share it with. Then I remembered this attractive, beautifully coiffed young girl, living almost under the same roof, who—'

'I've had enough remarks about my appearance for the day,' Jane said dryly. 'I'd love to come for supper, but what about Dad?'

'I've just tucked him up in bed with a plate of scrambled eggs and a glass of milk. Doctor's orders, I told him.'

'My, you have been busy...and clever! He would never have taken that from me.'

'Well, you're still his little girl. He can't change...any more than you can.'

He was looking down at her with a strange, enigmatic smile. 'You can change your appearance, but you're still the same inside—I hope.'

Her heart started beating faster. 'So you approve of the real me?'

'You're a much more sensitive person than you seem on the outside. I was watching you this afternoon, coping with your father's remarks, and I could tell you were hurting inside. I thought your father was somewhat insensitive in talking about your old boyfriend.'

She stood up and walked over to the window to gaze out across the fells, hoping the tranquil view would make her feel a little calmer.

'Oh, you mean Paul,' she said in a nonchalant voice. 'I'd forgotten all about him.'

'No, you hadn't!'

Richard was standing right behind her. She turned.

Gently, he leaned forward and put his arms around her. Jane tensed as her head told her resist. But her heart won as she moved into the circle of his arms. Looking up at him, she saw the tenderness in his eyes.

'You don't have to pretend with me, Jane,' he said, his voice husky with emotion. 'You might be able to fool your father but with me it's different.'

'Yes, I think it is,' she said softly, almost to herself.

He pulled her closer and bent his head to cover her lips with his own. His kiss deepened as he felt her response. She moulded herself against him, revelling in the hard contours of his athletic body. Desire flickered deep down inside her. She could feel herself melting, losing control...

'Come over to my place,' he whispered, as he broke away.

She was glad the inquisitive Lucy didn't come in for evening surgery as they went together, hand in hand, across the courtyard.

'What about Dad?' she said, as he released her hand so they could climb the old stone steps that led to his flat. 'Suppose he needs me?'

He put a hand in the small of her back. 'Stop worrying! He's got a phone beside his bed and I've told him to call me if he needs anything. I said you would be tired after evening surgery and needed your rest more than I did.'

Jane turned at the top of the stairs. 'You've thought of everything, haven't you?'

Richard gave her a slow, steady smile. 'I thought it

was time we had an evening all to ourselves. But I wasn't sure you'd agree to being abducted at such short notice.'

'I like surprises—they're usually more fun than things that have been planned for ages.'

He closed the door behind her and took her in his arms once more. She breathed a heavy sigh. This was where she belonged, in Richard's arms. Or rather, this was where she would like to belong! Because nothing was certain. Their relationship was an ephemeral, temporary situation that couldn't possibly last. But she was going to enjoy every moment while it did...

Her mind vaguely registered that there were food packages on the table as he led her through into the bedroom. He'd invited her for supper but the electric emotions that were travelling between them made it obvious that food was the last thing on their minds.

He reached for the buttons in the hollow of her neck. Slowly he bent his head and teased her bare skin with his tongue. She moaned and moved closer so that she could experience his arousal against her body. He tossed her new silk blouse and the flimsy lace bra over a chair, his hands gently caressing her breasts, moving slowly to tantalise her until she felt as if she was turning into liquid fire.

They moved on to the bed, his body over hers, his hands teasing, tantalising, driving her wild with a desire that demanded consummation. She gave a deep sigh as their bodies became one, moving slowly together, then with an urgent desire for fulfilment...

Jane touched his cheek. Richard looked so boyishly handsome in sleep. He moved, opened his eyes and reached for her again. This time when they came together their joint ecstatic experience was more profound. It was as if in exploring each other's bodies they had probed the inner depths of their souls and blended into one perfect, indivisible entity.

The moon was shining through the open window when she woke again. The room was lit only by moonlight. She put out a hand to the other side of the bed but she was alone.

'Richard?' Like a child waking in unfamiliar surroundings, she needed the reassurance of his presence.

He came back into the room almost immediately, putting on the light beside the bed. Jane saw that he'd pulled on a pair of jeans, but his broad, muscular chest was still bare. Smiling down at her, he reached forward and caressed her hair affectionately.

'It seems as if I've said goodbye to the new hairdo,' she said wryly, turning her head sideways to lay her face against his hand. 'It would have had to be sprayed with concrete to survive tonight.'

'It looks wonderful! I felt intimidated by that set look you had when you came in this afternoon.' He grinned. 'I mean yesterday afternoon.'

She pulled herself up into a sitting position. 'What time is it?'

'Two o'clock in the morning. Supper's nearly ready.'

'Good. I'm starving.'

Richard gave her a long, slow smile. 'I thought you might be. Come on, get up!'

He pulled her, protesting, from the rumpled bed and crushed her against him. She became suddenly aware of her nakedness. Stupid to feel shy after all they'd experienced together but she held back, looking around for something to throw on.

Her new clothes were scattered across the room.

Richard released her from his arms. 'There's a spare

robe in the bathroom. You've just time for a shower if you'd like one.'

Standing under the warm cascade of water, Jane remembered the tingling, erotic sensations she'd experienced with Richard. Nothing in her life had prepared her for a night like this! She smoothed shower gel over her body, feeling almost reluctant to wash the skin that he'd caressed.

He was putting the finishing touches to their supper when she arrived in the kitchen. She tied a knot in the belt of the huge towelling robe as she padded, barefoot, over to the cooker.

'Mmm, something smells good!'

'Grilled steak and microwaved chips,' he said. 'Would you like to toss the green salad in this French dressing I've made?'

Jane leaned over the large wooden bowl on the table and poured in the prepared dressing. Picking up the carved wooden salad servers, she began to toss the lettuce leaves with the herbs, oil and garlic.

'Haven't seen these salad servers before,' she said, as Richard joined her at the table, putting a plate of steak and chips in front of her.

'I've brought a few of my own things with me. Not much. Most of my stuff is over at the farm. There's no point having to move it all out twice.'

The delicious steak she was chewing seemed to lose some of its piquant flavour. 'Are you planning to move?'

'Well, I can't stay here for ever, can I?'

She didn't see why not! It seemed an idyllic situation, but she refrained from voicing her opinion as she reached for the salad bowl.

'So where are you planning to go?'

'I'm hoping to buy a house in the area. I've already looked at a couple. One in particular appeals to me.'

Jane could tell by his cautious tone that he was holding something back. 'Oh, really? Which house is that?'

'Fellside.'

She almost choked on her steak. Reaching for her wineglass, she took a sip before facing him across the table.

'Fellside was where Paul lived,' she said in a dull voice.

'I know,' Richard said quietly. 'But it's the finest house on the market at the moment.'

'But isn't it too big for a bachelor?'

'I don't intend to remain single for ever.'

'But what's the rush? Another equally fine house will come on the market when you...when you need it.'

Jane realised she was talking too quickly, clutching at straws—anything to stop him buying the house that had come to symbolise her humiliation.

He took a sip of wine, put down his glass and faced her across the table. 'So you really don't want me to buy Fellside?'

'It's got nothing to do with me,' she said quickly. 'You're the one who's going to live there. It hasn't got any bad memories for you.'

'Would you like to talk about it?'

'No!' Jane faced him defiantly, but as she saw the look of concern in his eyes she changed her mind. Sharing her memories with Richard might help to ease the pain. He was a very sympathetic listener.

'OK,' she said in a quiet voice. 'I made a complete fool of myself with Paul. I should have known I was way out of my depth with a worldly-wise man like him. But he seemed so charming and we got on so well. He was fun to be with…at first…'

'And then?' he prompted gently.

She took a deep breath. 'I couldn't understand why he asked me out in the first place. It was soon after he'd moved in to Fellside. He phoned Dad and invited the two of us to supper one evening. I was flattered by the attentions of this older, sophisticated man and Dad seemed to like him. He talked all the time about his travels and it was an interesting evening. Dad invited him back to our place the following week and from then on we saw a lot of each other.'

'And you didn't suspect anything?'

'Not at that stage.' She stared at him. 'Why did you say that? Do you know something about him that I don't?'

'My father is a lawyer. When I told him I was thinking of buying Fellside, he gave me details about Paul Drew which he learned from a legal colleague who'd dealt with the sale of the house. Apparently Drew was convicted of fraud in Australia and served a prison sentence. Afterwards he came to England for a short time until the dust had settled. His estranged wife tracked him down and persuaded him to go back with her.'

'She was his wife?'

'Yes, and she had no means of support other than Paul. She threatened to expose other shady deals he was into if he didn't go back with her and settle his debts back home.'

'I lent him money,' she said hoarsely. 'He told me he had a cash-flow problem. Something about contacting his bank in Australia. He promised to pay me back as soon as this bank draft came through but…'

'But he didn't?' Richard stood up and came round to her side of the table, putting his arm around her shoulder.

Jane leaned against him, breathing deeply. 'I drew ten thousand pounds out of my deposit account. My mother had left me some money in her will and the interest had grown over the years. How could I have been taken in like that?'

'You mustn't blame yourself. You'd fallen into the hands of a master crook. Dad says he's already wanted again by the police in Australia but they can't find him.'

She stood up and put her arms around his chest so that she could feel the comforting vibes of his sympathy. He bent his head and placed his cheek against her hair.

Jane groaned. 'I can certainly pick 'em, can't I?'

'Present company excepted, I hope?' he quipped.

She looked up into his eyes. 'I certainly hope so.'

Even as she said it she felt a pang of apprehension. She'd been in this vulnerable situation before, infatuated with someone who had the power to break her heart. What made her think that Richard would be any different?

'I'm obviously not a very good judge of character,' she said quietly.

Richard tightened his arms around her. 'You've just been unfortunate in the men you've been out with. Paul is a professional conman. Anyone would have been taken in by him. I can see that Fellside would have unhappy memories for you, but don't you think it would help to lay the ghost if you went there again?'

She shook her head. 'I don't want to have anything to do with the place! That part of my life is a closed book.'

'But you're still keeping it there at the back of your mind,' he said gently. 'If you were to go into the house, look around, see that the memories couldn't hurt you any more.'

She moved out of the safe circle of his arms. 'Richard, buy the house if you want to but don't expect me to set foot in it—'

The phone started ringing. Richard picked it up on the second ring. Jane could recognise her father's faint voice on the other end of the line. She took a step forward but Richard put his finger to his mouth.

'Now, don't worry. Just keep absolutely still, Robert. I'll be with you in half a minute.'

He was already reaching for his sweater.

'What's the matter?'

'Your father's got a pain in his chest and some breathlessness. He said he didn't want to waken you so he phoned me.'

She felt a guilty pang that she hadn't been over in her own room. But then she reasoned that her father wouldn't have disturbed her anyway.

'I'll follow you,' she said anxiously.

Jane's fingers were all thumbs as she pulled on her clothes. Richard was already crossing the courtyard. She closed the outer door of the flat and hurried down the steps, praying that her father's condition wouldn't deteriorate before they arrived.

CHAPTER SIX

RICHARD was bending over her father when Jane arrived, his hands moving over the older man's thin chest. The intense pallor of her father's face worried her.

'Dad? What's the matter?'

Robert looked up and gave her a wan smile. 'I'm only a retired old doctor. You two are the experts. There's this damn big pain, like somebody's sitting on my chest and...' He paused for breath. 'And the old lungs aren't working too well.'

He broke off and stared at Jane with a puzzled look on his pallid face. 'Why are you all dressed up like a dog's dinner, Jane?'

She'd pulled on the new trouser suit that had been draped over a chair in Richard's flat. The hours it had lain there had added a few creases and she realised that it must look strange for her to appear in her father's bed-room dressed like this in the middle of the night.

'When I phoned Jane, I said we might have to take you to hospital,' Richard said quickly. 'Which is what I intend to do. My guess is the wire in your pacemaker has become dislodged. I've examined the lump in the fatty tissues of your chest where they inserted the pacemaker after your cardiac arrest and it now feels slightly irregular to me. It was still *in situ* when I checked it this afternoon but it must have begun to work loose.'

Robert grunted disparagingly. 'That's Henry Gregson's handiwork! Calls himself a cardiologist!'

'Well, it doesn't usually happen, Dad,' Jane put in

soothingly. 'Most pacemakers are fine until the batteries need changing.'

She reached for her father's old brown dressing-gown and slippers. 'Let me help you into this and then we'll get you down to Moortown General...'

Her father grumbled as she started helping him to dress. The pallor on his face had now turned to an ominous flush. A well-equipped ambulance would be a safer form of transport but in the time it took to get one out here they could all be down in the safety of the hospital.

Jane breathed a sigh of relief as the old familiar outline of Moortown General Hospital came into view not long after that. How many times had she turned into the space where the ambulances parked with a sick patient? They always ticked her off but this time it was her own father who was giving her cause for concern so parking rules were the least of her worries.

She glanced in the driving mirror to where he was lying across the back seat, his head on Richard's lap. Richard's car would have been quicker but the tiny back seat wasn't practical. He'd phoned ahead to alert the accident and emergency and cardiology departments.

A porter with a stretcher, two nurses and the A and E duty officer came out to the car as soon as Jane stepped out of the car.

'If you give me the keys I'll park the car in the car park, Dr Jane,' the younger of the nurses said.

Jane recognised her as one of her patients who lived in Highdale. She tossed over the keys. 'Thanks, Kerry.'

Her father had lapsed into unconsciousness as they lifted him onto the trolley.

'Oxygen!' Richard said, clamping a mask over her father's face.

'The cardiac arrest team is on its way, sir,' the second nurse said. 'And we've phoned Mr Gregson.'

Inside A and E, the cardiac team took charge. Suddenly Richard and Jane weren't required any more in a professional capacity. From the detailed instructions Richard had given over the phone to Henry Gregson's senior registrar, the team had deduced that the problem with the pacemaker would have to be investigated and they had already set up one of the operating theatres for an emergency operation.

Jane held her father's hand in the ante-theatre. He was lapsing in and out of consciousness. She looked up, relieved, as Henry Gregson walked in.

A couple of nurses waited to help him into a theatre gown and mask. Jane introduced the cardiologist to Richard.

'I gather you think the wire to the pacemaker might have become dislodged?' Henry Gregson said tersely.

Richard nodded. 'Dr Crowther seems to be experiencing pacing failure.'

'Has Robert been sedated?'

The anaesthetist confirmed that he had.

'Good. Well, we'll give him a local anaesthetic,' the cardiologist said. 'And then I'll take a look at him in Theatre. Shouldn't take too long to replace the wire if that really is the problem. Half an hour, maybe an hour at the most. If it's something more serious, it'll take longer, of course.'

He glanced at Jane. 'Don't look so worried, Jane. Your dad's going to be OK. Why don't you go off and have a coffee in the medical residents' sitting room? You'll only get under my feet if you're waiting around here.'

Jane nodded. 'I'll leave my mobile number, Henry.

You'll get someone to phone me as soon as you've sorted out the problem, won't you?'

'Of course. Your dad's in safe hands. Now make yourselves scarce. I've got work to do…'

Richard took hold of her hand. The touch of his fingers was comforting but she had to steady her nerves to stop trembling with anxiety.

'I wish we could go in there with him,' she said quietly, as they walked out into the corridor. 'That's the trouble with having an old family friend in charge of the operation. I used to call him Uncle Henry when I was small, but I dropped the ''Uncle'' bit when I considered I'd grown up. But he still treats me like a child.'

Richard smiled. 'It's for your own good that he's asked you to leave. How much use would you be in the state you're in?'

'Not much,' she conceded. 'Caring for your relatives is always much harder than looking after patients.'

She shivered as she left the warmth of the theatre block.

'It reminds me of chilly nights spent trawling the corridors from one ward to the next during my time as a house officer,' she said.

She stopped still in the middle of the corridor. 'I'd better phone Caroline to tell her what's happened.'

'Don't you think it could wait until morning?'

She glanced at her watch, before pulling her mobile from her pocket. 'It is morning on Caroline's farm. Someone will be up and about, getting ready to do the milking.'

Over the phone she had to reassure her sister that their father was in no immediate danger, but Caroline insisted she was going to get dressed and come to the hospital immediately.

Jane began to feel calmer as they went through the swing doors that led from the hospital to the medical residents' quarters.

'Haven't been down here for years,' she said, as they started to descend the stone stairs that led past the bust of Alexander Fleming.

She had a sudden fleeting memory of the first time she'd met Richard, face to face.

'We once passed on these very stairs,' she said shyly, glancing up at him.

Richard looked puzzled. 'Did we? Not surprising really. It's a busy thoroughfare. Did something happen?'

She drew in her breath but remained silent. How could you tell a man that you'd fallen in love at first sight? The event obviously hadn't registered with him.

'Did you scowl at me?' he asked, a wry smile on his face.

'Why should I?'

'Since I came to work at Highdale I've been trying to remember my days at medical school. Some of the memories are slowly coming back and there's one abiding image of you that keeps flashing through my mind. Every time I saw you, you were frowning at me.'

'Only after you asked me out for a date and didn't turn up.' Jane paused at the bottom of the stairs and looked up at him.

His eyes held a puzzled expression. 'So that was the reason, was it? I've been wondering about it.'

'I thought you would have put two and two together and known why I was annoyed with you.'

He leaned forward and put his hands on her shoulders. 'Jane, I have no recollection of even asking you out, let alone not turning up. But so many of my earlier memories have been eradicated from my mind. After Rachel died it was as if a curtain came down. I seemed to lose my long-term memory completely. Most of it has come back over the years, but the unfortunate incident when I hurt you is still lost in the mists of time.'

He took her hand and led her along the corridor towards the medical staff sitting room. 'But, then, I was a completely different person in those days. Looking back now, I feel as if it all happened to a younger brother.'

'We've both changed,' she said quietly, as Richard pushed open the door.

'Coffee's still strong,' he said, handing her a cup from the cafetière that simmered permanently on the hob.

She cleared a space among the debris of medical journals scattered along the sofa so that Richard could sit down beside her.

'I really am sorry I hurt you,' he said quietly.

She took a sip of her hot coffee. 'And I'm sorry I scowled at you all the time.'

He leaned forward, took the coffee-cup from her hands and kissed her, oh, so gently on the lips.

Jane revelled in the feeling of closeness. The memories of their love-making only hours before came flooding back. But as she heard footsteps outside on the stone floor of the corridor, she pulled herself away, quickly.

The door opened. A tall, bald man in a white coat came in, giving them a cursory glance. She watched, surreptitiously, as he filled a cup with coffee and sank down into one of the battered old armchairs.

Something in his manner told her that he'd recognised the intimate rapport between Richard and herself as they sat close together on the ancient sofa. And there was also something in the way he'd swaggered across to the chair that was jogging her memory. She felt sure they'd met before. Well, he was one of the medical fraternity so it was very likely.

All she could see was the shiny skin on the top of his head as he buried himself in one of the medical journals. She noticed that Richard was now standing up, moving across the room to take a closer look at the stranger.

'Simon?' he said.

Jane felt a jolt of revulsion. Not Simon! Not the rat who'd blatantly two-timed her so that it had been common knowledge on the hospital grapevine, and then had had the nerve to ask her to take him back! He'd assumed they would carry on as if nothing had happened but she'd soon put him right on that score! Nobody treated her in that cavalier fashion and got away with it! She'd been hurt and humiliated and she'd made it quite clear she'd never wanted to see him again, so it had been a relief when he'd left the hospital soon after he'd taken his finals.

Looking at him now, it was difficult to recognise him without his long, fair hair, but, yes, she could see it was really Simon.

He was standing up now and she could see he'd put on weight round the middle. Probably a beer belly. He'd always liked his drink.

'My God! It's Richard Montgomery.'

His loud, raucous voice hadn't changed. What had she ever seen in him?

'I thought you looked familiar,' Simon was saying to Richard. 'When did you join the staff here?'

The two men were pumping each other's hands. She remembered they'd been great friends at medical school Her emotions were churning inside. She'd long since recovered from her attachment to Simon but the painful memories still lingered. She'd felt so humiliated when she'd had to explain to her friends that she'd no idea where he was and that she'd no intention of trying to track him down if that was the way he wanted it.

'I'm a GP based out at the Highdale Practice,' Richard said. 'We've just brought in Jane's father because of problems with his pacemaker. He's in Theatre at the moment. You remember Jane, don't you, Simon?'

Momentarily, Simon's face registered embarrassment before he recovered his composure and put out his hand towards her.

'I certainly do. What are you up to at the moment, Jane?'

She shook the limp fingers, made eye contact with those grey, shifty eyes and wondered how on earth she could have imagined, however briefly, that she had been in love with this man. And in a blinding flash she remembered that, having been hurt by Richard, she'd turned to Simon to help her to forget.

'I'm the other partner at the Highdale Practice, Simon,' she said quietly.

He was studying her carefully. 'So you two finally got together after all. Funny how things work out. Are you…?'

He gestured between them, making his searching question perfectly obvious.

'We're professional partners,' Jane said tersely.

'Maybe we could get together for a drink some time. I mean all three of us,' he added hastily. 'You're looking great, Jane. The ugly duckling turned into a swan if I may say so.'

'Thanks for the ugly duckling bit,' she said dryly.

'Well, you know what I mean. I never thought of you as being pretty, but look at you now!'

'So, what are you doing here, Simon?' Richard put in quickly.

'I've been working in a hospital in the States, but I got fed up working my socks off to support two ex-wives, not to mention the aggro they were both putting me through. So I upped sticks and came back to my favourite part of the world and signed on with a medical agency. I'm hoping to get a job on the staff soon but meanwhile, with less money coming in, it means I don't have to pay the wives as much and I don't have to listen to their endless bleating.'

'Love 'em and leave 'em, eh?' Richard said quietly. 'You haven't changed.'

Simon gave a sheepish grin. 'Why should I?'

Jane turned away and walked over to the door. 'I think we should go back to Theatre, Richard.'

He followed her, sensing her discomfort. 'Might see you around, Simon,' he called over his shoulder.

'I'll give you a call out at Highdale,' Simon said.

'Please, don't!' Jane whispered under her breath.

Richard put an arm round her shoulder as they went out into the corridor. 'I gather he's not one of your favourite friends from the past.'

She slowed her agitated pace to enjoy the comfort of being close to him.

'You know, it's been a momentous night. I feel as if all my yesterdays have come back to haunt me. First you tell me you want to buy Felldale and we start discussing Paul, and then Simon walks in, as cool as a cucumber, without a word of apology for making a fool of me.'

His arm tightened around her shoulders as they began to climb the stone steps. She paused by the bust of Alexander Fleming and looked up at Richard.

'Not to mention the fact that when I was eighteen and

I passed you on the stairs round about this spot I got an enormous crush on you.'

He stared down at her. 'Was it that bad? I'd no idea.'

No, he hadn't! And she certainly wasn't going to tell him how painful it had been. She'd said more than she'd meant to already.

She started moving upwards again.

'But I thought you were Simon's girlfriend,' he said gently.

'Simon and I were just good friends to begin with. Then, after you'd let me down, he sort of...sort of comforted me. Told me not to worry. Plenty more fish in the sea...that sort of thing,' she finished off quickly, realising she was babbling to hide her embarrassment.

'And he started being more than just a good friend, did he?' Richard said slowly. He was beginning to have an idea about what might really have happened all those years ago. Simon was perfectly capable of anything if it was in his own interests.

'Like I said, he comforted me. And one thing led to another. He could be very persuasive. After a while I really thought I was in love with him.'

Jane swallowed hard as she remembered how grateful she'd been that Simon had helped her to forget that Richard hadn't wanted her. And now, after all these years, just when she thought she'd come to terms with the situation, Simon had turned up to remind her of her unhappiness.

'I think Simon and I need to have a little chat,' Richard said evenly, pushing open the swing doors that led into the hospital. 'There are a few questions I need to ask him.'

She was alarmed by his serious tone of voice. Looking

up at him questioningly, she saw the intense expression on his face.

'What do you mean?'

He pulled her to one side to allow a porter and a nurse in charge of a patient on a trolley to go past them.

'I'll be able to tell you more when I've spoken to Simon,' he said quietly.

They arrived back as her father was being wheeled into the ante-theatre. He looked drowsy but his eyes were open and his face was a good colour.

Jane hurried over and took hold of his hand. 'How are you feeling, Dad?'

'Like I've drunk a couple of large whiskies, but I'm not complaining.'

'I should think not, Robert!' Henry, following the trolley, leaned over his old friend and patted his hand. 'Talking of large whiskies, I think that's the least you owe me when I come round to see you. Calling me out in the middle of the night like that! No consideration for my beauty sleep, have you?'

'It would take more than sleep to make you beautiful, Henry,' Robert said.

Jane felt relief flooding through her as she recognised that her father was getting back to normal again.

'So, was it a dislodgement of the pacemaker wire?' she asked the cardiologist.

'Certainly was.' Henry glanced at Richard. 'Good diagnosis. I've only had that happen once before.' He looked down at his patient. 'Have you been doing physical jerks or something? Taken up aerobics, have you?'

'Dad insists on vigorously digging in the garden,' Jane put in quickly.

The cardiologist pulled off his gloves and tossed them

in the direction of a bin. They missed and a nurse retrieved them.

'Well, you can cut that out for a start, Robert!' he boomed. 'I said you could go walking over the fields, not digging ditches.'

The swing doors flew open and Caroline rushed in, looking anxious and flustered. She was wearing a pink trouser suit and high strappy sandals.

'I came as soon as I could. Dad, how are you?'

'Your father is trying to recover from his operation, Caroline,' Henry said dryly. 'So don't start getting him over-excited. You never were one for being calm, were you?' He glanced over at Jane. 'It's getting a bit crowded in here. Why don't you take your sister to the ward so that you can all wait there for your father?'

Jane nodded in agreement. A nurse started to lead them away. Caroline began to cry as soon as they got out into the corridor.

'Dad looks so ill. What happened?'

'He's going to be fine, so don't worry,' Richard said as he began to explain the course of events since they'd found her father collapsed in bed.

'It's a good thing the two of you were there to help him,' Caroline said, drying her eyes on a tissue. 'Oh, damn, my mascara's running. I'll just slip into this loo and fix my make-up. Tell me which ward we're going to and I'll find it.'

They carried on down the corridor without her.

'You two are so different,' Richard said quietly. 'Imagine finding time to put make-up on when she was worrying about your father being brought into hospital!'

Jane gave a wry smile. 'Caroline wouldn't be seen dead without her war paint! She's worn it since she was about twelve but I could never get the hang of it myself.

It was then I realised that I could never look as chic as she did.'

'Thank God! I wouldn't want you to change.'

The nurse had already left them, having indicated the ward at the end of this particular deserted stretch of corridor. Richard stood still and put his arms around her.

'Stay just the way you are, Jane. I love the new hairstyle, but the old one suited you just as well. It's the sum total of your personality that I find so...so fascinating.'

As he looked down at her he could feel the tender emotions churning inside him. He could hardly dare to believe that it was love blossoming, but he recognised the symptoms. He'd thought it wouldn't be possible to love again after the trauma of bereavement but the emotions he felt for Jane were unmistakable. This was more than simply the joy of wanting to make love to a desirable woman.

But how could he convince someone who'd been badly hurt before that she could dare to trust again? Even as she looked at him now, he could tell that she was worrying about something. She had that far-away expression that told him she daren't commit herself.

Richard lowered his head, longing to kiss her, to soothe away some of the pain he saw in her eyes.

There was the sound of a trolley behind them. He straightened up and continued walking. It would take time and patience to gain her trust. But he was already formulating a plan...

CHAPTER SEVEN

'WHAT glorious heather!' Jane ran a hand through her ruffled hair as she marvelled at the endless swathe of dusty pink carpet that covered the high moorland.

Richard smiled as he steered the car up on to the top of the hill. 'I love the heather but it means autumn is just around the corner.'

'Not for ages yet! It's only July. We're still in the middle of high summer. It's going to be a perfect day.'

As she spoke an ominous cloud covered the morning sun. She felt a pang of apprehension. It seemed to symbolise her relationship with Richard. Her father's emergency operation a month ago had seemed to draw them closer together. Everything was going so well between them, but she knew, from her past unpleasant experiences, it couldn't last. Sooner or later...

Richard gripped the steering-wheel as they turned off the main moorland road down the bumpy track that led to their patient's house.

'What did Alan actually say on the phone this morning, Jane?'

Jane pulled herself up straight in the passenger seat as she tried to remember the exact words.

'It was his friend Diane who phoned. She's got a very blunt manner and she didn't seem as if she wanted to divulge any details. She simply asked if we'd both go over as soon as possible. I asked her if Alan was all right and she said she'd explain when we got there. She didn't want to talk over the phone. To be honest, it was like talking to MI5.'

'And you're sure she wanted both of us to go?'

'Yes. She was quite adamant about that.'

She smiled to herself as she remembered scooting upstairs to change as soon as she'd finished morning surgery. These new cotton trousers and shirt were professional enough for a visit to Alan's house and casual enough if they stopped off for lunch in a country pub on the way back. She knew just the place where, with any luck, there wouldn't be anyone from the Highdale area.

The first thing she noticed about Alan's house, as Richard switched off the engine, was that someone had given it a lick of paint. And there were clean floral curtains peeping from the sides of the windows again, just as it had been when his mother had been alive.

It was Diane who opened the door. There was a large apron tied over her jeans and T-shirt and she had a screwed-up duster in her hand.

'Oh, you came,' she said bluntly. 'Alan's been waiting for you.'

Jane stepped onto the newly washed kitchen floor. 'You didn't say it was urgent.'

'Mind yourself on that slippery floor! It's not urgent, but Alan's an impatient beggar and once he sets his mind to something…'

'Well, you were just as bad, Diane,' Alan said, moving forward to greet them as they all went through into the living room.

'My, what a transformation!' Richard looked around him in admiration. 'Someone's been busy.'

Diane smiled. 'We did it together. I don't intend to let Alan get lazy even if he's not as fit as he should be. Any excuse to get out of a bit of work.'

Jane was delighted to see the bright new paintwork and the clean covers on the sofa and chairs.

'Diane made all the covers and curtains out of some material my mother had stashed away in the loft,' Alan said proudly. 'We've washed them but Diane is convinced they still smell of mothballs. Would you like some coffee?'

'No coffee, thanks,' Jane said quickly, curious to find out what the problem was without any more delay. 'So, how've you been, Alan?'

'Fine! This new beta interferon must be doing me a lot of good. I'm walking a lot better so...' He looked across at Diane.

'So Alan's asked me to marry him,' she said quickly.

For a few seconds Diane's announcement with all its implications for the future was hard to digest. Jane was pleased, but at the same time she was thinking of the uncertainty surrounding the progress of any patient with multiple sclerosis.

Richard was looking across at her, waiting for her to say something, because, after all, she'd known the couple longer than he had.

She smiled across at Diane and Alan. 'That's great news! I hope you'll both be very happy.

Diane smiled back. 'That's why we've asked you here this morning. Alan insisted we get your approval before we go ahead.'

Richard moved across the little room and sat down beside Diane. 'You don't need our approval,' he said gently.

'If the two of you love each other enough to make a lifetime commitment then you must go ahead. But as you know, there is a lot to consider and prepare for. Alan knows his condition will probably worsen as time goes by so he won't mind me saying this. The sheer physical effort of looking after a sick husband can put a tremendous strain on a marriage.'

'I've explained all this to Diane,' Alan said quietly. 'She knows what she's letting herself in for, but she's a very tough character and it hasn't put her off, has it?'

'No, it hasn't,' Diane said firmly. She looked across at Jane. 'You see, I've loved Alan a long time now. We first went out together when we were still at school. But when he first told me he'd been diagnosed with multiple sclerosis I panicked. I couldn't bear to think about it so I simply ran away.'

'I remember you leaving the shop in the village,' Jane said. 'Someone said you'd gone travelling the world.'

Diane gave a wry smile. 'I stayed away nearly two years, just meandering around, taking a job where I could get one—waitress, shop assistant, fruit picker… I wanted to forget Alan, to find my own life. Oh, it was so cruel of me, but he's forgiven me, haven't you?'

Alan smiled. 'Yes, I don't blame you. I would probably have done the same myself.' He looked across at Richard. 'But I've told Diane that she can take off any time it all gets too much for her. I want to marry her but at the same time I won't hold her back if she gets fed up.'

'I won't take off again,' Diane said firmly. 'Especially if we have children.'

'That's something we wanted to ask you as well,' said Alan. 'We'd love to have children, but were worried about the risks.'

Jane looked at Richard. The fact that she'd known this couple longer than he had was hindering her professional assessment.

'Medical research is divided about whether the multiple sclerosis gene can be handed down from parent to child,' Richard said carefully. 'We'll make an appointment for you to see your neurology consultant at the hospital so that you can ask him about it and make your decisions. But for now I'd like to offer you my congratulations, and we both wish you all the luck in the world.'

'Thanks, Doctor,' Alan said quietly. 'Somebody once said that love conquers everything. I firmly believe that.'

'It's absolutely true,' Richard replied, his voice husky with emotion. He turned to look at Diane, whose eyes had misted over as she'd listened to Alan's sentiments. 'You know, I went through a bad patch when I simply drifted around, trying to forget someone, so I know what you were going through.'

Diane leaned forward to listen more intently. 'Do you?'

Jane held her breath as she saw Richard's enigmatic expression. Was he going to reveal his tragic past in front of Alan and Diane?

'It wasn't quite the same for me because there was no possibility of me going back to how it was, but I still needed to find myself,' he said quietly.

'And did you find yourself, I mean?'

'I think so. Time and travel are great for sorting out your problems and showing you who you really are and what you really want, but you need a lot of help when you come back to the real world.'

'Alan has helped me to get over feeling guilty at running away,' Diane said evenly.

'You mustn't feel guilty, Diane,' Richard told her. 'You're probably a much stronger character now than before you went away, and this will mean you'll give one hundred per cent to your marriage.'

'Are you stronger since you went away, Doctor?' Diane persisted.

Richard cleared his throat. 'I certainly know what I want from life.' He stood up and walked over to Jane. 'I think we should be going now.'

She stood up, her emotions in turmoil. Listening to Richard just now had given her an insight into his true character. A man with such firm beliefs in the power of love couldn't be simply enjoying a no-strings-attached affair until he tired of her, could he? Because every time they made love that was exactly what it felt like. Making love! Not simply having sex for the sake of slaking their lust, mind-blowing as their sexual encounters were.

She could feel tremors of excitement beginning deep inside her as she remembered how tender he was, coaxing, teasing, loving…yes, really loving.

She took a deep breath of the heady moorland air as she tried to clarify her thoughts. Had Richard's traumatic experiences really changed him from the person he'd been in his happy-go-lucky medical schooldays when he'd seemed to be tarred with the same brush as people like Simon?

'You'll both come to the wedding, won't you?' Diane said as she showed them to the door. 'I've got to sort out the licence and everything as soon as I can. Now that we know we've got your approval. We're going to try for a date in August. No point in waiting when we both know our own minds.'

Jane turned at the door and took hold of Diane's hands. 'If we're free on the wedding day, Diane, we'll definitely come. I'm really happy for you.'

Diane smiled. 'Thanks. You've set my mind at rest.'

She was still standing on the step, waving happily, as they drove away.

'Thanks, Richard,' Jane said quietly. 'You handled that really well. I was rather concerned at first as I don't want to see either of them hurt.'

'There are medical obstacles to overcome but they can do it. They're going to live together, whatever happens, anyway, but they'll find that marriage is something special. I think they're very lucky to have found each other. Alan and Diane seem made for each other and that isn't something that happens in every marriage.'

'I hope you're right.'

'You're very sceptical, aren't you, Jane?'

'I prefer to think I'm cautious where matters of the heart are concerned,' she said carefully. 'If Diane has left Alan once, there's nothing to say she won't do it again, especially when the going gets tough.'

Richard was frowning. 'Look, you can't go through life letting what happened in the past colour the way you handle the future.'

She bridled. 'It's called the wisdom of experience, Richard, and I happen to believe that if you're once bitten you should be twice shy.'

Jane leaned back to let the cooling breeze blow through her hair. It had grown over the weeks so it was almost touching her shoulders again. But with a little extra brushing and daily shampoos she was keeping it under control. And Richard had told her only last night as she'd lain in his arms that he loved running his hands through her hair. So that was a good enough reason for putting off another dreaded encounter with the scissors.

Neither of them spoke for a few minutes. This was the way most of their arguments ended. They simply agreed to differ.

He was slowing down the car at the top of the hill that led down into Highdale. 'Can I buy you some lunch?'

She smiled. 'You certainly can. How about the Coach and Horses?'

He nodded. 'That's along the crest of this hill, if I remember rightly.'

'Yes, they haven't moved it. I took Paul in there once but he wasn't impressed. He called it a spit-and-sawdust kind of place. He was more at home in a five-star hotel.'

'So long as someone else was paying,' Richard said dryly.

'True! But I didn't know I was paying at the time,' she said slowly.

He pulled up in front of the ancient pub which had weathered the storms of numerous Yorkshire winters. The wooden tubs at the front gave it a festive air and the strong July sun twinkled on the narrow panes of glass.

Jane thought it looked a welcoming kind of place as she turned to open her door.

Richard put his hand over hers and leaned across. 'I've asked my father to see if he can do something about getting your money back from Paul,' he said quietly.

She stared at him. 'Richard, there's absolutely no chance he'll be able to track him down. You said yourself that no one knew where he was. Besides, I've come to terms with my loss so—'

'No, you haven't. It's festering at the back of your mind, along with all the other humiliating baggage you're carrying around with you. My father is a brilliant lawyer. He's got legal contacts in Australia. I just wanted to make sure you would approve of him making enquiries on your behalf.'

'I think it's a wild-goose chase…' She hesitated. That sounded so ungrateful for efforts that were being made on her behalf. 'I'm grateful that your father is even considering this, but even if he succeeds in making contact with Paul he won't be able to get a penny out of him.'

'The law is on your side, Jane. Leave it with me. That's one problem I hope we can solve. The sooner we get it out of the way the sooner you can start living again.'

She felt a surge excitement running through her. 'I thought I was living. What do you call this? A summer's day, a handsome escort to my favourite pub...'

Richard leaned forward and kissed her slowly, gently on the lips. She wanted to swoon into his arms but the practicalities of the situation inhibited her. People were leaving their cars, swarming into the pub, casting surreptitious glances at the smart sports car with its interesting occupants.

One or two of these people might be her patients and they would be sure to recognise Richard's distinctive car.

'We'd better go inside and get a table,' Jane said quickly.

They sat beside the huge inglenook fireplace. The landlord had removed the fire basket and logs in deference to the summer weather, replacing them with a small fountain that cascaded over coloured stones. Jane gazed into the illuminated water feature, enjoying its beauty but at the same time thinking how much more cosy it was in the winter when someone would toss a log onto the fire.

She turned to watch Richard getting the drinks at the bar and wondered how their relationship would have progressed in a few months' time when the wind would be howling over the fells. The present was about as blissful as it could get, but nothing ever stood still. If only she could keep their relationship in this state of limbo for ever, she would be happy.

Jane checked her thoughts, knowing that wasn't strictly

true. Deep down inside her she knew that she wanted more. She wanted to be able to look into the future and see herself with Richard for the rest of her life...

'I've ordered you the dish of the day,' he said, putting her glass of wine down on the table. 'There was such a crowd clamouring for food I thought I'd better get our order in quickly.'

She smiled and raised her glass. 'Thanks. What's that you're drinking?'

He pulled a face. 'One of their drivers' specials. Non-alcoholic ginger something or other. Oh, and the dish of the day is home-made steak and kidney pudding.'

'Great! There's nothing like good, wholesome Yorkshire cooking.'

'My sentiments exactly.' He was watching her over the rim of his glass. 'You haven't got a clinic this afternoon, have you?'

Jane shook her head.

'I haven't got anything planned until my evening surgery, so why don't we go for a walk over the fells?'

'Sounds good to me.'

The food was a long time coming but they both agreed it was worth the wait. As soon as the last mouthful had been finished, Richard stood up, impatient to be out in the fresh air.

He drove the car further along the crest of the hill and parked in a fellside field, carefully closing the gate behind him to keep in the sheep who were always likely to wander down and endanger themselves on the road.

They climbed the path steadily, pausing briefly to catch their breath before resuming their trek. The view from the top rewarded their efforts. They sat, leaning against each other, turning their heads to look in all directions at the panorama of hills, fields and the ribbon of river snaking along the valley beneath them.

They began to descend the path that led through the pine forest at the other side of the fell. The cool shade of the trees was welcoming but the pine needles scattered over the dry path made the descent hazardous.

'Careful!' Richard, walking behind Jane, put his hands on her waist to prevent her from falling as she began to skid.

She stepped back, feeling much more secure in his arms. 'Thanks, I nearly…'

The closeness of her body had triggered his desire. He turned her to face him, pulling her even closer.

A current of passion sparked between them. Her pulses raced as he took her hand, leading her away from the treacherous path into the fragrant, pine-scented forest. He stopped walking beneath a tall, majestic tree, its branches sweeping down to the ground.

Jane leaned back against the trunk of the tree. It was like a secret house. She felt safe as she gave herself up to the rain of kisses that Richard was showering on her face. She tugged impatiently at his shirt, longing for the feel of his skin against hers. He lowered her to the ground, his hands caressing her skin. She moaned with pleasure as he explored her body with tantalising fingers.

She had no idea how long they lay there, touching, exploring, caressing, intent on delaying the longed-for climax but knowing that the delicious waiting game added to the heightened ecstasy of consummation…

Jane opened her eyes and looked up at the leafy branches. The air felt cooler. She must have slept after experiencing their ecstatic love-making. Each time she made love with Richard she thought that they'd reached the ultimate heights, but inevitably the next time always surpassed the previous experience. She propped herself up on her elbow and watched him sleeping as peacefully as a little boy. His hair was rumpled over his forehead, his mouth turned up as if he was smiling.

Maybe he was remembering in his dreams. Jane touched his lips with her finger and he opened his eyes. He reached for her and she went willingly into the circle of his arms.

But she was aware that time had passed and they had to get back to the real world.

'We ought to go back,' she whispered, dragging herself away from the lure of unreality, that other world she longed for where men were eternally faithful to the women who loved them. She sighed. The dream was over until the next time.

If indeed there was to be a next time. She never allowed herself to look too far ahead. It was asking for trouble if you expected too much.

Richard hauled himself upright and pulled her to her feet. 'Before we go, I want to ask you something,' he said quietly.

She looked up at him, intrigued by his serious tone.

'I've had another look at Fellside and it's just what I'd hoped for as a home. Will you come and see it with me?'

'Richard, I don't want to go into Paul's house ever again.'

'It's not Paul's house now. And if you were to put the past behind you and look at the place in the clear light of day, that would be one piece of unwanted baggage cleared out from your subconscious.'

Jane bridled. 'Ah, so that's what all this is about, is it? You're trying out your psychology on me, aren't you?

Always telling me to move on and forget the past. Well, I've tried and I can't, I simply can't.'

She resented the tears that were now trickling down her cheeks. She felt so weak, so vulnerable.

He pulled her back into his arms, his hands caressing her back with gentle, tender strokes. 'I'm sorry I mentioned it. I didn't mean to upset you. Forget it, Jane. I won't speak about the house again. OK?'

Richard moved back, holding her at arm's length, his eyes searching hers.

She nodded. 'OK, I didn't mean to react like that but Fellside to me means Paul... And Paul...' She shuddered.

Gently, he wiped her cheeks with a clean white linen handkerchief, dabbing carefully at her eyes.

'Good thing you don't wear mascara,' he quipped, pulling a wry face as he put the crumpled handkerchief back in his pocket.

Jane laughed, welcoming the release of tension. She had a sneaking suspicion that maybe Richard was right to tell her to confront her fears from the past. The idea certainly conformed with the psychology lectures she'd attended on the subject. But she'd never thought any of it applied to her. It was just a load of theory. Maybe she was wrong not to go along with Richard on this. But, if she was, she didn't want to admit it—not yet, anyway!

Jane moved around the sitting room, switching on the little lights, as the evening sun cast dark shadows over the garden. Her father was still struggling with his *Telegraph* crossword puzzle. He'd started it that morning and had complained bitterly that the clues were getting harder. She put her hand on his shoulder and looked down at the paper.

'Four across is—'

'Don't tell me! I'll get it in my own good time. The old brain isn't what it used to be but there's no need to rub it in.'

Jane patted his shoulder affectionately. He hated the fact that all his faculties were slowing down. But at least they'd sorted out his cardiac problems. His physical health was better than it had been for ages.

She glanced at the clock as she moved back to her chair. Richard would finish surgery soon. She wondered what he was doing this evening besides the paperwork he'd said he was going to work through.

'Did you invite Richard in for supper?' her father asked, as if reading her thoughts.

'Richard knows he doesn't need an invitation.'

Her father's face fell. 'So you didn't ask him?'

'He said he would be busy with some paperwork this evening,' she said quickly.

'That's no excuse. A man must eat. You two haven't had a row, have you?'

'No! Of course not.'

'I thought you were getting on rather well. Nicest chap we've had around here for ages.'

'Praise, indeed!'

His shrewd eyes were watching her. 'You like him a lot, don't you?'

Jane hesitated. 'He's an excellent doctor and a very good friend,' she said carefully.

'Well, I should be a bit careful with him. Hold back a bit. Just keep him as a colleague and a good friend. I mean, we wouldn't want any complications, would we? I only hope he won't do anything to upset you… I mean, if he gets fed up with being a country doctor and wants to spread his wings.'

She drew in her breath. Why did her father have to

reinforce her fears? The implied assumption in this family was always that Plain Jane couldn't keep a man for long.

'Richard is free to come and go as he pleases,' she said evenly. 'If he decides he wants to move on I won't try to stop him.'

She sat very still, willing herself to stay calm as the awful idea of living without Richard took hold. A feeling of bleak desolation engulfed her. She knew that when the inevitable happened her heart would shatter into little atoms that would take years to piece together again.

But she would cross that bridge when she came to it. She stood up. 'I'll go and help Mrs Bairstow in the kitchen.'

She leaned out of her bedroom window to get a better look at the new moon. It was bad luck to look at it through glass. The scent of the roses that Alf meticulously tended was everywhere on this calm summer night. It had been such a perfect afternoon out there on the fell. But now it seemed light years away. Even a few hours without Richard brought her back to earth and set her feet firmly back on the ground.

Supper had been a quiet affair, her father making an effort to eat the specially prepared chicken in a cream sauce and Mrs Bairstow chiding him when he left too much on the side of his plate. Jane had secretly hoped Richard might turn up for a coffee and a nightcap with her father as sometimes happened.

He hadn't even phoned her as he often did when she was back in her room. She would have pretended she hadn't been expecting his call, before making her way quietly across to his flat.

Maybe she ought to listen to her father's advice and

hold back a bit. She was too available. But if she held back she would be denying herself. If this was the only time she was going to spend with Richard then that was what she would settle for.

Her phone rang. Jane hurried to her bedside table. When it wasn't Richard's voice her spirits dropped.

She put on her professional voice. 'Yes, Jane Crowther here. Ah, Mrs Branson, how can I help you?'

A mental picture of her plump, harassed-looking, fifty-year-old patient came into her mind. She'd been treating Mrs Branson for depression for some time now. She was a good-natured woman, who'd taken on too many family commitments and was bending under the strain.

'It's Judy, my granddaughter, Dr Jane. She's locked herself in the bathroom.'

Someone was tapping on Jane's bedroom door. 'Just a moment, Mrs Branson.' She covered the mouthpiece. 'Come in.'

Her pulses raced as Richard walked in. He'd never come to her room before, probably in deference to the fact that her father was sleeping in his bedroom at the other end of the landing.

He closed the door and leaned against it. 'Your phone was engaged.'

'I'm speaking to a patient.'

'I can wait.' He sat down on the bed.

'Sorry about that, Mrs Branson. Can't you persuade Judy to unlock the bathroom door?'

Richard leaned forward. 'How about sending for the fire brigade?' he whispered.

Jane covered the mouthpiece again. 'Shh, she's very upset.'

Richard's eyes immediately registered concern. 'I'll help if you need me.'

She nodded. The distraught grandmother was saying that her granddaughter was screaming now but still refusing to open the door.

'I'm not strong enough to break it down and there's nobody else in the house. I hope she's not taken some of those awful drugs you read about. I've checked that bottle of pills you gave me for my depression and she hasn't taken any of those.'

'I'll be with you in a few minutes,' Jane said, putting down the phone.

Richard insisted on coming with her. 'It could be drugs,' he said, as he drove quickly out through the iron gates of Highdale House. 'In which case she'll need medical help.'

'Or it could be something quite different,' Jane said thoughtfully. 'Locking yourself in the bathroom, screaming loudly…'

She considered that line of thought carefully. It certainly was a possibility even though Judy was only thirteen. She hoped she was wrong. Judy's grandmother would be devastated. After her persistent depression, a big shock could push her over the edge.

'Mrs Branson has looked after Judy since she was a toddler,' Jane told Richard. 'Judy's mother wasn't married and the father didn't want to know anything about the baby. A couple of years later the mother got married and her husband said he didn't want to be saddled with a toddler, so Grandma Branson took her in. Grandpa Branson got fed up with his wife spending all her time looking after a fractious child and went to live with a young widow in Moortown. Then Judy's mother and her new husband moved down to London and I don't think they ever took any more interest in Judy.'

'Some women have an impossible life. How's Mrs Branson coping?'

'Not very well at the moment. I only hope history isn't repeating itself tonight.'

'What do you mean?'

'Judy locked in the bathroom could be screaming because she's giving birth. It's only a suspicion but we can't take any chances.' She pulled her mobile from her bag and punched in the digits. 'I'm phoning for an ambulance.'

'But wouldn't the grandmother have noticed if she was pregnant?' Richard said, as Jane finished speaking to the hospital.

'She's always been an overweight child. Grandma believes in comfort feeding. A few extra pounds could well go undetected.'

Richard screeched to a halt in front of the rambling farmhouse on the edge of the moors. Jane grabbed her medical bag and followed him up the path to the kitchen door. It was flung wide open. Mrs Branson, wringing her hands in despair, stood to one side to allow them to go in.

Richard took the stairs two at a time. Taking a deep breath, he hurled himself at the bathroom door. There was a creaking sound but it held. Again he put the full force of his shoulder against it and this time the lock caved in.

Jane swallowed hard. Her assumption that Judy was in labour had been correct.

'It's OK, Mrs Branson, we'll take over now,' she said gently, blocking the distressing sight from the grandmother's view.

'I don't want Gran in here or that man!' Judy screamed.

Richard led the worried grandmother along the landing to her bedroom while Jane got on with what had to be done.

'Give me a shout when you need me,' he called over his shoulder.

The young girl was lying on her back, her eyes rolling desperately. She clutched at Jane's hand. 'I'm having a baby, aren't I?'

'It's almost here, Judy,' Jane said. 'No, don't push. Try to pant like this...'

Judy was now panting desperately.

'Good girl, yes, that's the way. Now you can stop for a bit.'

Jane was carefully manipulating the baby's head out through the fully dilated birth canal. She carefully checked to see that the umbilical cord wasn't curled around the baby's neck. All was well. No complications. The next contraction should expel the baby.

She grabbed a couple of towels, putting one to stem the flow of blood and mucus that was trickling onto the floor and placing the other under Judy's head.

'I thought it might be a baby,' Judy sobbed quietly. 'That's why I didn't want Gran to know. Ah-h...'

Now wasn't the time to tell the young girl that the secret couldn't be kept from Grandma any longer.

'You can push now, Judy,' she told her, willing the frightened young girl to have the strength to expel the baby.

Jane eased the tiny shoulders out of the birth canal and then took the rest of the baby's body as it slithered out in a final slippery rush. Carefully, she placed the baby on Judy's stomach as she reached inside her bag for some surgical scissors.

'You've got a little girl, Judy,' she said gently, as she cut the umbilical cord.

The young girl's eyes widened. 'Can I...can I hold her, Doctor?'

'Of course you can. She's your baby.'

Carefully, she wrapped the precious bundle in a clean towel. As she handed the tiny infant to the new mother she felt a pang of deep emotion. The first precious moments in a baby's life, when the beginning of the mother and baby bonding process occurred, had never ceased to fill her with wonder. The sheer delight in the young mother's eyes was in stark contrast to the howling, terrified agony of the birth.

'She's beautiful, Judy,' Jane said.

'I didn't mean to have her, but now I'm glad I did. I tried all sorts of things to make my period come. I kind of hoped it would all go away.'

'Babies don't go away.'

'It's funny, I've been hating this lump inside me and trying to get rid of it, but now that it's turned into a real baby I love her, I really do...'

Tears were rolling down the young mother's face, splashing onto the baby who was now wailing loudly.

'The ambulance is here, Jane.' Richard's voice from the other side of the door gave her a sense of relief. She could hand over to the obstetric department. This was one young mother and baby who were going to need a lot of tender loving care.

'I really don't know what to think, Doctor Jane,' the new grandmother said a few minutes later, as the ambulance swayed round another corner. 'It's all such a shock. You see, I've been through it all before with Judy's mother but I never suspected I'd have to go through it again. I mean, Judy's only a child herself. At least her mother was seventeen.'

The young mother who'd caused the upheaval in Margaret Branson's life remained silent, clutching her newborn baby to her breast. In the most natural way, the infant had begun suckling immediately and Judy was completely fascinated by the process.

Jane leaned across from her seat next to Richard in the ambulance so that she could show Judy how to support the baby's head. Judy looked up from the baby and smiled.

'I can't believe it!'

'Neither can I!' her grandmother said. 'You'll have some explaining to do, young lady.'

'Not now, Mrs Branson,' Jane said quietly. 'Judy's coped very well but she's very tired.'

Richard leaned across and patted Mrs Branson's hand. 'Judy isn't really taking anything in at the moment. She's in a world of her own. But when reality sets in we'll give you all the help we can. You mustn't feel you're on your own because there's a good support system in this area. And Jane and I will come out to see you if ever you need us.'

'Thanks, Doctor. You've been very kind. I don't know what I would have done without you when Judy was screaming like that.' She glanced across at Jane. 'You're very lucky to have found such a sympathetic man as your partner.'

'I know,' Jane said.

'Are you going to be with the Highdale Practice permanently, Dr Montgomery?' Mrs Branson asked.

Richard's eyes held an enigmatic expression. 'Nothing

is ever permanent, is it? I'm here for the foreseeable future.'

Jane swallowed hard as she wondered how long foreseeable was.

CHAPTER EIGHT

'RICHARD, I don't believe it!'

Jane rushed into his consulting room, waving an envelope.

'I was sorting through the post, trying to get it out of the way as quickly as possible, when I opened this astonishing letter.'

Richard stood up and led her over to the chair beside his desk. 'Sit down, Jane. You look as if you've seen a ghost.'

'I have! A ghost from the past. Paul has actually written to me and—you'll never believe it—he's sent me a cheque for ten thousand pounds! Richard, I've got my money back. Do you know what he says in the letter…?' Her voice trailed away. 'You knew, didn't you? Is this all thanks to your father?'

He nodded. 'Dad told me that negotiations were under way. He had a legal expert working on it out in Australia. Apparently, when he caught up with Paul he discovered that he wasn't as impecunious as we thought. Somehow or other he's solvent again so when we threatened him with legal action if he didn't pay back his debts…'

'But Paul could have insisted the money was a gift, couldn't he?'

'Not with his record of taking women for a ride. You're not the only poor soul to have been charmed and then fleeced by him. Besides, the cashier at the bank at Moortown where Paul cashed the cheque was suspicious and had made a note of the circumstances.'

'Yes, I remember they actually rang me up to see if the cheque was genuine.'

'So if he'd tried to contend it in a court of law his arguments wouldn't have been believed.'

'But hasn't all this cost your father a lot of money? I ought to pay him something for his professional services.'

'He wouldn't dream of taking a penny,' Richard said vehemently. 'Dad regards this as a favour he did for a friend. It was the principle involved that intrigued him. He can't bear it when someone he knows has been taken for a ride.'

He paused and his expression softened. 'You know, my parents took a shine to you that day when we dropped in for tea. They keep asking when I'm going to take you to see them again.'

She shifted in her chair and looked away from him. 'Did you tell them we've been really busy at the surgery?'

He gave a wry smile. 'Why do I get the feeling you don't want to go?'

Jane drew in her breath. Richard had suggested a visit to his parents' farm a couple of times before and she'd made some excuse. Last time they'd gone over to Deepdale, the day when Sean had nearly drowned, she hadn't been so heavily involved with him. She'd been able to be dispassionate about the situation. But now that she was head over heels in love she felt they would sense it. And if they started asking questions about their relationship—as all parents did—she would be so embarrassed.

Their affair was one thing; parental involvement would only complicate things. But how could she explain that to Richard?

'I'd love to go,' she said, trying to sound convincing. 'But I really am busy at the moment. We've got to take time off to go to Alan and Diane's wedding tomorrow...'

He nodded resignedly. 'Don't worry. I get the picture.'

'I'd like to go over and thank your father some time,' she said quickly. 'I'll write him a letter today. It really feels as if a great load has been lifted from my shoulders. The times I've thought about that scheming rat and wondered why I'd been such a fool to be taken in by him. But now you tell me he was a master of deception. I'm sorry for all the other poor women who were taken in, but it makes me feel a lot better.'

Jane picked up the letter again. 'Do you want to know what Paul says?'

'Can't wait to hear.'

'He actually says he's sorry for taking so long in paying me back. He'd always meant to but he'd lost my address.' She laughed. 'That's a bit feeble.'

'Let's say Paul has always been a bit economical with the truth. Well, now that you've got your money back and he's apologised, do you think you can put that unfortunate chapter in your life behind you?'

She smiled. 'I hope so. All I know is that a load has just rolled off my shoulders.' She paused as a disturbing thought crossed her mind. Since last month, when she'd told Richard that she didn't want him to mention Fellside ever again, she'd been wondering if she was overreacting. As Richard had pointed out, it was only a house. Paul didn't live there any more. And it happened to be a house that Richard was extremely interested in.

'I've been wondering if you've made any more progress towards buying Fellside,' she said slowly.

He shook his head. 'Haven't given it a thought. I expect it's been sold by now.'

'But you were so adamant that you liked it.'

'I did, until you put me off. I began to think you knew something that I didn't and that maybe there was something wrong with it. Anyway, I know you don't want to talk about Fellside so—'

'I've changed my mind.' She gave him a wry grin. 'Woman's prerogative.'

Richard leaned across and put one finger under her chin. Slowly, he bent his head and kissed her on the lips.

She savoured the moment, feeling the thrill of excitement running through her as it always did when their lips touched.

'What an enigma you are, Jane,' he whispered huskily. 'I'll never be able to understand what goes on in that complicated head of yours. That's what I love about you, the unpredictability.'

She held her breath as he pulled away. He'd used the word 'love'. And his voice had sounded so tender. Even if he was only talking about a quirk of her character it gave her hope that their relationship was moving on to something more permanent...

She pulled herself up sharply. That kind of reasoning would only lead her into unhappiness. She was coming to terms with the past and enjoying her life in the present. It would be disastrous to make predictions about the unknown future.

But she felt a sudden fixation for Fellside. She simply had to go and see it now that the situation with Paul had been sorted out.

'I'd like to see Fellside again,' she said evenly.

'I'll find out if it's still on the market.'

The intercom on Richard's desk buzzed. Lucy announced that Mrs Branson, his first patient, had arrived.

Jane stood up. 'Grandma Branson seems to have taken

a liking to you, Richard. She used to come and see me but now she's your patient, I gather.'

He gave her a wry smile. 'She poured out her heart to me that night Judy had her baby.'

Jane turned back, her hand on the door. 'And you're a good listener.'

'It goes with the job.'

She held open the door to allow Mrs Branson to come in.

Their patient smiled. 'Oh, hello, Dr Jane. I've brought Judy and baby Alice with me. Lucy said she'd try to fit her in on your list.'

Jane could hear a baby crying in the waiting room and made the decision to see the new mother and baby first. The other patients wouldn't relish having to endure the baby's cries as they waited.

Going to the waiting room, she smiled at Judy as she took the baby from her arms. 'I'll see you now, Judy.'

'Alice is hungry, Dr Jane,' Judy explained as soon as they were alone in the consulting room. 'I didn't have time to feed her properly. Gran was in such a hurry to set off and I didn't want to miss the chance of coming to see you when she would be in the other consulting room, seeing the other doctor. Every time I wanted to come over she said she would come in with me and I didn't want that. She still treats me like a child.'

Jane settled the baby with her mother. Judy lifted her T-shirt and the hungry baby latched onto her breast with a contented sigh.

Looking at the young mother, Jane thought it was incredible that she could have produced this beautiful baby at such a tender age.

'Your grandma can't help treating you like a child, Judy,' Jane said carefully, trying hard not to antagonise the precious rapport that had built up between them since she'd delivered the baby. 'She's looked after you since you were very small, and that doesn't seem so long ago to her. The fact that you're now a mother hasn't made you any more grown-up in her eyes.'

Judy fixed trusting, childlike eyes on Jane. 'You know, it's so strange being a mum. I feel so much older than my friends now. They keep coming round to see the baby, asking if I'm going to take Alice to school with me, and to be honest...' She broke off and, holding the baby over her shoulder, proceeded to rub her back until the baby gave a loud burp.

'Good girl,' she said lovingly, as she put the baby to her other breast. 'As I was saying, all these questions they ask me, I don't know half the answers myself.'

'I've been onto Social Services,' Jane said. 'So someone should have been to see you about your future education and—'

'Oh, yes, a couple of women came to see me, but I wanted to see what you thought. They've told me I can go to a special educational unit in Moortown where I can take the baby with me, but I don't want to leave my old school. I didn't want to ask Grandma if she'd look after Alice.'

The phone on Jane's desk rang. It was Richard, asking if she could spare him a couple of minutes. Mrs Branson had a problem he thought she could help with.

'I've got to go next door, Judy. Will you be OK for a minute?'

Judy grinned. 'Take as long as you like. Alice is a greedy little girl. Going to be as fat as your mum, aren't you, darling?'

Mrs Branson was frowning when Jane went into Richard's consulting room. 'Has Judy said anything about going back to school, Dr Jane?' she asked as soon as the door was closed.

'We'd just started to discuss it.'

'I thought that was what she wanted to talk to you about. She never tells me anything. I know she wants to go to this special unit but I'd rather keep the baby at home with me during the day and have her go back to her old school.'

Jane stared at her. 'But why didn't you tell her this?'

'She loves that baby so much I don't think she can bear to be parted from her. She never lets me do a thing for her. But to be honest, I love looking after babies. It's when they start growing up I find them difficult. I just haven't got the patience to put up with their cheekiness. Judy was lovely till she was about ten and then...' Mrs Branson raised her hands. 'Such a little madam!' She leaned forward to emphasise her point.

'I think helping to look after baby Alice would be just what I need to start getting closer to Judy again. I always wanted another baby after my daughter started growing up but my Bert couldn't stand children. I was really happy to look after little Judy but Bert went off to live with his fancy piece in Moortown and—'

'I think it might be a good idea,' Richard put in quickly, knowing from past experience that Mrs Branson in full flow could talk the hind leg off a donkey.

'I think that sounds like a good idea,' Jane said encouragingly. 'And by the time baby Alice starts growing up Judy will have finished school and will be able to take care of her herself.'

Mrs Branson smiled. 'Yes, I thought of that. I mean, I'm only fifty now, but I wouldn't want to be looking after Alice when I go down the village for my pension.'

Richard looked at Jane. 'Do you think that Judy would like to come in here and discuss the situation?'

'I'll go and prepare the ground,' Jane said evenly.

As she went back into her consulting room she was thinking that it was a pity the lines of communication had broken down between grandmother and granddaughter. It was up to Richard and herself—and baby Alice—to re-establish contact.

It took a great deal of persuasion on Jane's part to get Judy to agree to a supervised discussion with her grandmother. But once they had both aired their views and found they were both steering in the same direction, the atmosphere in Richard's consulting room became more relaxed.

Judy clutched little Alice against her protectively. 'You'll let me look after her when I come home from school, won't you, Gran?'

Grndmother Branson bridled. 'You'll be welcome to her by then, my girl. Looking after a baby is going to be no picnic, I can tell you. I'm only doing it for your sake so…'

'I really do appreciate it, Gran,' Judy said, with exactly the right amount of deference.

Jane smiled at her, glad that she'd pointed out to Judy that although her grandmother loved looking after babies she was going to have to make sacrifices in her way of life.

'Well, I think we've got that sorted,' Richard said. 'We'll let the authorities at the special unit know that you won't be requiring a place.'

'Thanks, Dr Montgomery,' Mrs Branson said, standing up and indicating to her granddaughter that it was time for them to go.

As the door closed Jane turned to Richard. 'Maybe this

is the start of a permanent state of peace between those two.'

Richard nodded. 'Everything was bound to be a compromise, but I think this should work.' He paused. 'Has Judy told you who the father is?'

'Yes, and as you're my medical partner I can breach the confidentiality rule. Apparently, it's one of the boys at school and they don't like each other any more. She thinks he would deny it if he was asked.'

He frowned. 'Tricky situation, this one.'

'I can't break Judy's confidentiality. She'd never trust me again if I did. If she chooses to tell her social worker what she told me then it's not my problem.'

He came towards her and took hold of her hands. 'Trust is a very fragile commodity. It can be shattered so easily.'

Jane swallowed hard as she looked up into his enigmatic blue eyes. If only she could trust Richard not to break her heart. She'd given so much of herself but there was still a tiny part of her that she didn't dare to surrender.

She pulled away. 'I'd better go or the patients will be queueing outside.'

'I'm going over to Deepdale for lunch. My parents would be delighted if you came with me.'

She turned at the door. 'Sorry, I've promised Dad to drive him over to Caroline's.'

It was true, but she was glad of the excuse. Given the turbulent state of her emotions, she knew she wouldn't relish being under scrutiny by Richard's parents.

The Highdale church organist was working through his wedding repertoire as Jane looked for a suitable pew. Richard, who'd driven her from the house, had been delayed as soon as he'd set foot in the churchyard by a couple of young community nurses who'd wanted to discuss the patients they were working with. Jane had walked on and left him to it, because it was obviously Richard they wanted to talk to.

Looking back when she reached the church porch, she saw that the small group had been augmented by two nurses from Moorfield General. Richard was smiling and talking in an animated fashion and the young women were hanging on his every word. What a charmer! All the girls obviously thought so. What on earth made her dream she might keep his attention for much longer?

The seats in the church were filling up rapidly. She caught sight of Caroline, gesticulating that there was room in her pew.

'Richard not with you?' Caroline asked, as Jane sat down beside her.

'He's talking to some people outside.' She held her breath as she waited for the next inevitable questions.

After lunch at Caroline's farm the previous day, her sister had made it obvious that she was worried about Jane's relationship with Richard. Their father was having a snooze on the sofa so the two sisters had taken their coffee out into the garden and Jane had been forced to fend off the searching questions posed by her sister.

'Jane, I hope you weren't offended by what I said yesterday. I really am warning you about Richard for your own good. You're very naïve where men are concerned and I'd hate to see you hurt again. You really seem to have fallen for him in a big way but there's nothing to say that this time will be any different from any of the others. I mean, after your affair with Paul—'

'Caroline, I wasn't offended yesterday,' Jane said through clenched teeth. 'But if you persist in going on at me today I might start screaming. So just shut up, will you?'

Caroline sniffed. 'Well, if that's going to be your attitude when I'm only trying to help so that you won't get hurt again…' She broke off as she noticed Richard standing at the end of the pew.

Richard greeted them both. 'If you move along, Caroline, I can sit here at the end of the pew next to Jane… That's fine, thank you.'

'Everything OK between you two?' he whispered as he sat down.

Jane rolled her eyes heavenwards. 'Everything's perfectly normal,' she said evenly. 'Attitudes never change in my family.'

She gave him a sideways glance and thought how handsome he looked in his grey suit. She had a sudden desire to become possessive! It was totally out of character for an independent soul like herself but she longed to slip her arm through his and make it clear to everyone that she was his partner. She wanted the whole world to know that they were an item! She'd had enough of a secret affair that couldn't go anywhere.

And to make matters worse, just when she was beginning to hope that this time it would be different, her wretched sister had to start stirring up her doubts and fears about the future.

She smoothed her hands over the cream silk skirt of her suit. It would have looked better if she could have found time to iron it. Sitting next to the most handsome man in the church, she wanted to look good. Caroline, on the other side of her, still managed to look as if she'd stepped from a page of *Vogue* in her dove grey, impeccably cut designer suit.

Alan, the bridegroom, was waiting for his bride in the front pew, ably assisted by his brother as best man.

As Diane walked down the aisle on the arm of her father, Jane thought she'd never seen such a transformation. Beneath the white veil she looked serene and untroubled as she drew near to Alan.

'A lovely wedding service,' Jane said to her sister as they walked out into the sunshine.

The music and the quiet responses of the couple in love had moved her to tears during the service. She was feeling completely benign now and ready to ignore her sister's well-meant but unwelcome remarks.

Caroline agreed that the service had been excellent. 'Jane, I hope you—'

'Sorry, Caroline. There's an old schoolfriend over there…'

The only way to deal with Caroline's doubts—and her own—was to ignore them!

Richard had followed her to the edge of the crowd. Together they watched the photographer snapping away, preparing the photographs for the wedding album.

'Alan and Diane were lucky to get the wedding organised so quickly,' Jane said. 'Apparently, there was a cancellation at the church and at the hotel reception.'

'Yes, I heard that one of the bridegrooms had called his wedding off.'

'It does happen,' she said quietly. 'Still, our lucky pair have been able to take advantage of it.'

'I reckon they are a lucky pair,' Richard said slowly. 'Oh, I know they've got Alan's multiple sclerosis to contend with, but they seem to have the makings of a lifetime's commitment. A rare thing nowadays when so many marriages are ending in divorce.'

He hesitated. 'I saw Simon last week and he was tell-ing me about his two divorces. Pretty traumatic, appar-ently.'

Jane looked up at him. 'I didn't know you were going to see Simon.'

'I rang him up and asked him to meet me for a drink.'

'You rang him? Why on earth did you do that? I would have thought—'

'He used to be my best friend, remember?'

'How can I forget?'

'What's that supposed to mean?'

'Sorry, Richard. I shouldn't take it out on you, but you know how I feel about Simon.'

'That was exactly why I arranged to meet him without telling you,' he said. 'But I'd like you to come with me next time.'

She pulled a wry face. 'I don't want to have anything more to do with him.'

'I think you would be interested in what he has to say. I certainly was.'

She stared at him, puzzled. 'What did he have to say that I could possibly be interested in?'

'You won't believe it unless you hear it from Simon. What night are you free this week? Thursday? Friday?'

'Friday,' she said slowly. 'But it had better be worth hearing if I'm going to spend the evening with that awful man. You are going to come with me, aren't you?'

He gave her a rakish grin. 'I might.'

'Dr Jane, Dr Montgomery!' Alan was gesticulating at them from the church steps. 'Diane and I want a photo taken with you two, please.'

Jane hurried across with Richard. The crowd parted to let them through. It was difficult to produce the required smile when she was desperately aware of her sister frowning at her from the front row of onlookers. She wouldn't stoop to glare at her sister when the photographs of the bride, groom and their two doctors had been taken. Couldn't Caroline see this was simply a professional photograph?

The bridegroom kissed Jane shyly on the cheek. 'Thanks for all your help, Dr Jane. That day when you came round I was so worried. I hadn't really decided to go ahead but when you and Dr Montgomery gave us your blessing it all seemed to fall into place. We've never looked back since then.'

Jane smiled. 'I'm glad it's all going well for you, Alan. You deserve it.'

'You're both coming to the reception, aren't you?' Diane asked.

'Of course,' Richard said.

The following Friday, Jane had suggested she drive so that Richard could drink beer with Simon.

'I don't mind sticking to orange juice,' she'd assured him. 'So long as you don't mind sitting in the passenger seat of my ancient Ford.'

Richard had tossed her the keys to his powerful black monster and, intrigued at the daunting prospect of turning herself into a prospective rally driver, she'd accepted his offer.

Now, as she steered the powerful car up the hill that led to the Coach and Horses, she wasn't so sure it had been a good idea.

'You'd better take it down a gear,' Richard said quietly.

She knew he was right but wasn't sure she could find the right gear on that fancy gearbox and steer round the approaching hairpin bend at one and the same time.

Especially with Richard watching her every move as he sat, rigidly, on the edge of his seat.

She took a deep breath and grasped the gear lever. Amazingly it responded in exactly the right way she'd hoped.

She smiled as she cleared the top of the hill and changed gear again. 'Nothing to it once you get the hang of the gears! You weren't scared, were you?'

He laughed. 'Of course not! I could see you were perfectly in control... There's Simon's car in front of the pub. Bang on time! Makes a change for Simon. He must be nervous.'

She switched off the engine. 'Why should he be nervous?'

'Just wait till you hear what he has to say. I can assure you I had to twist his arm to get him here at all. And it's going to take a few beers to lubricate him and loosen his tongue.'

'I don't think Simon should drive his car,' Jane said in a worried tone as Richard bought his extremely drunk friend yet another pint.

She was slowly becoming more and more bored and longing to escape the tedium of the two men reminiscing about old times in medical school as if she didn't exist. She'd declined any further orange juice and glanced at her watch pointedly.

'This will be his last pint,' Richard whispered, setting down the frothy brew in front of his red-faced, now incredibly garrulous friend. 'Then I'm going to call him a cab and insist he takes it—my treat!'

'You must have spent a fortune on him tonight,' Jane said, in a puzzled tone. 'Why?'

'Shh! Just listen to what he has to say now,' Richard

told her. 'Simon, remember what you told me the other night about my so-called date with Jane all those years ago?'

'That's history, Richard. You don't want to hear about that again.'

'Oh, but I do, and so does Jane, don't you?'

She nodded, intrigued. 'What date, Richard? We never succeeded in having a date, thanks to—'

'Thanks to Simon!' Richard said evenly. 'Go on, explain, Simon.'

Simon groaned. 'I don't know why you keep dragging this up,' he said truculently. 'I only did it for a bit of fun.'

'You might think it was funny, but I don't,' Richard said ominously. 'When you set up that date between Jane and me you knew she'd be upset and start looking for a shoulder to cry on, didn't you?'

Simon frowned and took another gulp of his beer. 'It's all so long ago, I've forgotten what I was thinking.' He glanced across at Richard. 'It'll cost you another pint, you know.'

'You've had enough. Just tell Jane what you told me last time we met.'

Simon focused his bleary eyes on Jane. 'That letter you got from Richard, asking you to meet him on the town hall steps…well, I wrote it myself…like I said, for a bit of fun…and, yes, I admit it, so that you would come running to me for a bit of comfort and…and whatever else happened along.'

He drank the dregs of his drink and held up the empty glass. Simon ignored him.

'You were a very feisty girl, Jane,' Simon said unsteadily. 'Vivacious and attractive in your own kind of way. Not everybody's cup of tea, but I fancied you rotten.

But you insisted on keeping me at arm's length, making it quite clear that we were just good friends. I was your buddy, the person you told your troubles to, but anything else was off limits.'

She stared at him in surprise. 'I'd no idea you felt like that about me.'

'Well, anyway, when you kept bleating on about how you thought Richard was so wonderful and you wished he would ask you out, I got jealous—hopping mad, in fact! So I thought of a way to shut you up and get you for myself...'

Jane drew in her breath. 'How could you?'

Richard put out his hand and took hold of Jane's to steady her. 'It was all a long time ago, Jane. I knew nothing at all about it.' He paused. 'Have you kept the letter I was supposed to have sent you?'

'You must be joking! I tore it into a thousand pieces on my way back from the town hall. It went into the nearest rubbish bin.'

'So it never occurred to you to check the handwriting?'

'Why should I? I didn't know what your handwriting was like and, anyway, in those days I still had a very trusting nature. When I discussed it with Simon he said he knew you'd sent a letter to me, and I had no reason to doubt him, whereas now...!'

She raised her eyes heavenwards.

Richard put his arm round her and drew her against him. Even in the crowded pub she didn't resist. Suddenly she felt she didn't care what people thought any more.

'All these years I've harboured a grudge against you, Richard,' she said quietly, looking up at him. 'I'm sorry.'

He smiled. 'Nothing to be sorry about, now that we've resolved the mystery. I honestly thought it was one of the incidents from the past that I'd forgotten when my memory blanked out after I'd lost Rachel. When you first told me about it, I thought what a swine I must have been! And I could understand why you'd glared at me every time we passed in medical school or the hospital.'

'When you two have finished chatting between yourselves, I'd like to get another drink before they close,' Simon said, waving his empty glass in the air. 'What you don't realise is that I'm celebrating. This is my final drinking session—I hope!'

Richard's eyes narrowed. 'What do you mean?'

Simon gave a sheepish grin. 'I'm going into a clinic to be dried out tomorrow. I was caught drinking on duty last week and I lost my job. So I've been told that unless I get dried out I'll never get another one. I started drinking heavily during my first awful marriage and it's been a problem ever since.'

Richard put his hand on his old friend's shoulder. 'I'm sorry, Simon. But you're doing the right thing.'

Simon pulled a face. 'I know.' He lifted his glass again. 'So, how about one for the road?'

Richard took the glass away from his friend and carried it over to the bar, before calling up the village taxi.

'Your cab's on its way, Simon,' Richard said, helping his friend to his feet. 'We'll all wait outside. A bit of fresh air wouldn't go amiss. The landlord says he'll keep an eye on your car tonight and I'll come and drive it back to the medical staff car park at Moortown General tomorrow if you'll give me the keys.'

Much later, Jane snuggled against Richard. Their love-making had been slow and relaxed, as if they both recognised that another problem had been resolved. Richard had insisted on driving the car back to Highdale House and Jane had thankfully handed over the keys after he'd pointed out that he'd only drunk one pint of beer during the whole evening. He'd confined himself to ginger beer after that so he could be sure Simon made a full confession.

'I feel sorry for poor old Simon,' she said, nuzzling her face into Richard's neck and thinking how she loved the scent of his aftershave mingled with that distinctive soap he used when he showered.

'He's only got himself to blame,' Richard said. 'He threw everything away. I only hope he can get his life back together again. He's got a tough time ahead but if he really wants to succeed he will. The trouble is, he hasn't got any incentive at the moment. He was telling me there was no one in his life who cares whether he lives or dies.'

He hesitated, his eyes moist, his voice husky. 'I went through a period when I felt completely alone. And you know what? After a while I didn't care. I was in a permanent state of nothingness. Just going through the motions of living, but feeling nothing.'

Jane stroked his cheek gently. 'That was nature's way of healing you, of making you whole again. When you felt strong enough you came back into the real world, didn't you?'

'But I was still searching... I still am...'

She'd never seen him so moved. She longed to cry out and tell him to stop searching, that she wanted him to stay with her for ever...

But she was afraid that if she put it into words her impossible dream for the future would shatter. So she turned her words into actions in the only way she knew that would give them both fulfilment and a feeling that, in the whole of the world, only the two of them existed.

She teased him, caressed him and revelled in the excitement of arousing his desire again. He moaned as she caressed him until he was gasping for fulfilment. And when they came together in climax she gave an ecstatic cry of wonder...

The thin light of dawn was showing through the window. Jane stirred and reached out to check that Richard was still there. He pulled her into the circle of his arms. They kissed, the long slow kiss of two lovers sated with a night of delirious passion.

'I'd better go,' she whispered.

'Stay and have a shower with me,' he whispered, his voice husky with renewed desire.

She smiled. 'If I do I'll never escape.'

'And would that be so bad, staying here with me in my little apartment?'

He broke off. 'I nearly forgot to tell you. I'm going to stay in the flat for another few weeks while I carry on house-hunting. I phoned up the estate agent to enquire about Fellside but it's under offer.'

Jane couldn't understand why she felt so disappointed. Was it because this had been the house that Richard had set his heart on until she'd put him off? Until she'd resolved her problem with Paul the thought of entering the place had been anathema to her. But now that it was unavailable she wished whole-heartedly she hadn't put up any opposition to Richard's plan.

CHAPTER NINE

JANE leaned back in her chair and looked out of her consulting-room window. The roses were beginning to wilt. They'd been a riot of colour throughout the summer but now, in the middle of September, Jane thought the garden was beginning to take on an older, sadder expression. Everywhere there were signs that autumn was nearly upon them.

Nearby, at the edge of the carefully tended lawn, she could see her father meticulously dead-heading the roses. As if sensing her eyes upon him, he raised his head and waved. She smiled and waved back.

There was a tap on the door and Richard came in. 'I'm just off on my rounds. Anyone else to add to my list?'

Jane shook her head. 'Look at Dad. He's as happy as a sand boy since we told him he could do some light gardening.'

Richard leaned against her desk. 'He's been a good old boy recently. I think that problem with his pacemaker in the summer made him start to take notice of our advice and realise he's not immortal.'

'Henry Gregson is very pleased with his progress. I spoke to him on the phone this morning when I was trying to get an appointment for a patient.' She smiled. 'I also had to phone the hospital about Fiona Smithson. She's our patient who had an ovarian cyst removed in the spring, remember? Well, I checked her over this morning and she's definitely pregnant. She's over the moon!'

'That's good news. Is she fully recovered from the operation?'

'I gave her a full examination and she seems perfectly fit so I was able to reassure her because she'd been wondering if they should have waited a bit longer.'

He stood up. 'I noticed young Sean, the boy who nearly drowned during the summer, waiting to see you. I didn't know he was one of our patients.'

'He's not. He just dropped in to bring us a present. Wasn't that nice of him? I've had a peep but I've wrapped it up again. Close your eyes, Richard.'

Richard grinned but did as he was told. Jane reached down under her desk to take hold of the elaborately wrapped parcel, before handing it to Richard.

He felt at the string. 'I'll have to open my eyes to get into this.'

'OK.' She smiled as she watched him fiddling with the brown paper.

He pulled out a small, elaborately carved wooden house.

'Sean said he made it himself at school in the woodwork class.'

'What a remarkable present! And he said it was for both of us?'

'He certainly did,' she said lightly. 'We'll have to take turns with it. I'll keep it this week and then you can have it for a while.'

She was staring at the tall chimney tops at either end of the carved wooden roof. 'It looks like Fellside. Sean told me he'd based it on a house he'd seen in this area.'

Jane ran her finger over the detail on the front of the carving. 'He's got the large front door to perfection.'

A shiver ran down her spine, as if a ghost were walking over her grave. It seemed as if the boy she'd saved from drowning somehow knew that Fellside was a significant house in her life.

Richard moved forward to take a closer look. 'I think you're right. What a coincidence! Especially as the estate agent rang me about Fellside only this morning.'

She stared at him, wide-eyed. 'But I thought you said it had been sold.'

'It was under offer, but the people have backed out. They couldn't raise enough money. So the estate agent wanted to know if I was still interested.'

Her heart was pounding inexplicably. 'And are you?' she asked with studied nonchalance. He raised one eyebrow, the expression in his eyes totally enigmatic. 'Do you think I should be?'

'Oh, yes!' Jane broke off, embarrassed by her spontaneous show of enthusiasm. It was only a house, nothing to do with her. But she had an indefinable hunch that it would somehow be a good omen if Richard bought it.

'I've made an appointment to see it again this afternoon.' He hesitated. 'You can come with me if you're free.'

'I'd like that,' she said quietly. She placed the wooden house on her desk. 'What a nice gesture to come and say thank you like that. Sean's a lovely boy.'

He smiled. 'Yes, he is. Not at all what I expected that day when we had to wade through the empty beer cans before we could start trying to save his life.'

She nodded. 'Talking of beer, have you heard how Simon is?'

'I phoned the unit yesterday. He's done four weeks and is completely dry. They want to keep him another two weeks but he's champing at the bit to get out again.'

'Poor Simon! I never thought I would feel sorry for him, but I do. He doesn't seem to have had much luck in his marriages. I think I've forgiven him for what he did to me. I actually imagined, in my naïve eighteen-year-old way, that I was in love with Simon. It could have been disastrous if we'd stayed together because, during the six months we were going out together, he had bouts of awful depression when he would snap my head off.'

'I've remembered a lot about him since we met up with him again. He once told me he'd had a rotten childhood,' Richard said. 'He was brought up in a children's home and had to work really hard to get his place at medical school.'

'He never told me that,' she said. 'In fact, he was never very forthcoming about his background when we went out together.' Jane hesitated as the memories flooded back. 'To be honest, he was the first person to rouse my physical desires and I imagined that was love.'

'And it wasn't the real thing, was it?' he said gently, his eyes searching her face.

She looked up into his eyes and swallowed hard. 'No, it wasn't,' she said, her voice wavering with emotion.

Now that she was experiencing the real thing she realised that it had taken her unfortunate experiences to make her appreciate the difference.

Richard looked down at her with tenderness in his eyes. 'You were unfortunate to meet someone like Simon when you were so young and inexperienced. He found difficulty in staying faithful to one girl for long. I remember him saying he wasn't going to stay on at Moortown because there were too many ties. He said he wanted to travel around for a while on his own, to escape all the commitments he'd had during his time at medical school and start a new life.'

She looked at him in surprise. 'So you can really re-member that period again?'

Richard nodded. 'It's all coming back, bit by bit. I feel as if I've been struggling with a giant jigsaw puzzle, but I think I've finally found all the pieces. It's been a very cathartic experience, meeting Simon again.'

'It certainly has,' she said vehemently. 'It's sorted out a few problems.'

He bent his head and kissed her gently on the lips. 'I've got to go.'

He turned at the door. 'I'm going to call in on Sara Holdsworth. She phoned Lucy and asked for a house call today or tomorrow. She said it wasn't urgent. Apparently, she's been having persistent backache and didn't feel like trekking over to see us. Well, she is eight months preg-nant, so I said I'd go over.'

Jane frowned. 'She's been as fit as a fiddle for the last few weeks. She had some backache round about six months but it was only because she was overdoing things, getting the house ready for the baby. She'd been painting and papering the spare room to make it into a nursery and I had to tell her to stop. You don't think this back-ache…?'

'Well, it crossed my mind she might be getting some early contractions but Lucy said she was adamant that there was no rush. If there are any complications I'll get her into hospital as soon as possible. I won't be able to tell what's happening until I've had a look at her.'

Jane stood up. 'I'd like to come with you. Sara's a bit shy and if she needs an examination she'd prefer me to do it.'

*   *   *

Sara's kitchen door was wide open.

'Sara!' Jane called as Richard closed the door behind them.

'I'm up here, Jane, having a lie-down.'

Jane went into the first room at the top of the stairs and looked with concern at the pale figure huddled beneath the duvet.

Jane put a hand on her patient's clammy brow. 'How are you feeling, Sara?'

'I was OK apart from this wretched backache. But since I phoned up this morning it's got a lot worse. I can't understand it. I've been taking loads of rest since you stopped me working on the nursery. Ray finished it off for me and made me put my feet up. But this morning I was reaching up to get some teabags from the top cupboard and I felt this pain in my back. I think I might have slipped a disc.'

'I'll take a look,' Jane said.

'It's all down here in my back,' Sara said, as Jane peeled back the duvet and put on a pair of sterile gloves.

'It's not your back that's the problem,' Jane said gently. 'I'm going to have a look down here and check if all's well in the baby department. Just relax while I...'

She straightened up and looked across the bed at Richard. 'Second stage dilatation,' she said quietly.

His expression mirrored her own. Not another emergency delivery!

Looking down at Sara, she explained that the baby had decided to come early and was already on its way.

'Your birth canal is almost fully dilated, Sara, which is what was causing the pain.'

'But I'm not due for another four weeks. It's going to be OK, isn't it? I mean— Ah-h!'

Sara clung to Jane's hand, biting her lip to ease the pain.

Richard was talking to the hospital on his mobile. He snapped off the connection.

'An ambulance is on its way and they're expecting Sara in Obstetrics, Jane,' he said, quietly.

Sara screamed out as she clung to Jane's hand. 'It's getting worse. What…?'

'I'll give you something to ease the pain, Sara,' Richard said, reaching into his bag for a syringe.

Sara wouldn't let go of Jane's hand. As soon as he'd given Sara the injection, Richard put on sterile gloves. He could see that the baby's head was already wedged in the birth canal. Carefully, he eased it out, until the tiny shoulders were in view. He checked that the umbilical cord wasn't round the baby's neck.

'You can push when you feel the next contraction,' he said calmly, running his fingers over his patient's abdomen so that he could anticipate the contraction.

'I can feel one coming now,' he told her. 'Take a deep breath and… Good girl!'

He took the slippery infant in his broad hands. Jane handed him a sterile dressing sheet from her bag to wrap around the bawling baby.

'It's a boy, Sara,' Richard told her.

'Oh, how wonderful!' the new mother said. 'Ray wanted a boy. He'll be so pleased.'

Jane had a fleeting image of that day, only three months ago, when she'd had to convince the reluctant father-to-be that he wanted this baby.

She handed the baby to Sara and felt a lump in her throat as she watched her delight.

'It's always so satisfying to see how babies bring their own love with them, isn't it?' she said quietly to Richard.

He nodded. 'The majority of unwanted babies become

wanted when they actually become a reality,' he said softly.

They could hear the sound of the ambulance arriving in front of the house.

'Will you both come with me to the hospital?' Sara asked anxiously.

Jane smiled. 'Of course.'

'This isn't the way back to Highdale,' Jane said, as Richard took a left turn off the main road from Moortown.

They'd settled Sara and her new baby into Nightingale Ward at Moortown General Hospital and Jane was already planning how she could best use her time after lunch at home.

'I'm taking you over to Deepdale for lunch,' Richard said evenly. 'I was going to go at the end of my house calls before Sara delayed me.'

'But Dad's expecting me back at the house.'

'No, he's not. I phoned him while you were talking to the sister on Nightingale. He said Mrs Bairstow was already preparing to serve the soup and it wasn't a problem. Then I rang my mother and she was delighted.'

'Well, I think you should have asked me before...'

'And have you tell me you were too busy?'

There was a wry grin on his face as he took his eyes momentarily off the road and risked a sideways glance.

She gave him a reluctant smile. 'I feel as if I'm being hijacked.'

'You are! And not before time! You're too stubborn for your own good.'

'But I'm scared, Richard!'

He drew the car to a halt in the wide gateway of the field. Leaning across, he took her in his arms. 'What's there to be scared about? It's only a lunch, for heaven's sake!'

'But I'm sure they'll sense that we're…that we're…'

'Lovers?' he said softly. 'Don't you think they already know that?'

Jane looked up at him sharply. 'Have you told them?'

'I didn't have to. Every time I went over I found myself talking about you. Mum asked me outright and I said, yes, we were having the most wonderful affair. I've always been able to talk to my mum. She's been more like a big sister than a mother.'

She swallowed. 'But you told her that was all it was…a temporary affair…?'

'As a matter of fact, I told her that was all I thought I could hope for…at the moment. I said you'd had some unfortunate experiences with other men and it would be some time before I could convince you that we might think about something more permanent.'

'Such as?' She could dream, couldn't she? This was the moment when he would surely back off…

'Such as marriage,' he said, his voice husky with emotion. 'Will you marry me, Jane?'

The world seemed to have gone silent. She wasn't aware of anything around her except Richard looking down at her with that tender, pleading look, as if he expected her to reject him. She was part of the dream she'd always hoped would become reality, and now that it had she didn't know how to handle it.

She closed her eyes as she tried to concentrate on her answer. Marriage was such a big step.

'Have you any idea what you'd be taking on?' Jane said, opening her eyes to look up at him once again.

He gave her a slow, tender smile. 'I've had nearly six months to get to know the most difficult, the most obstinate, the most interesting, most desirable girl in the world. Why do you think…?'

'No, I don't mean just me,' she put in quickly. 'I know you can handle me when you want to. Look at the way you've just hijacked me! What I meant was, do you know what a big commitment marriage is? Being with the same person for the rest of your life could be very—'

'Look, I've seen good marriages and bad marriages in my professional and my private life. My own parents have weathered over forty years together. I've heard them having big rows, Mum slamming the door and going into the kitchen to throw the pots and pans around. But before the end of the day, they've sloped off to their bedroom, hand in hand, and I always knew I mustn't disturb them. Marriage is what you make it…' His voice wavered.

'I'm sorry, Richard,' Jane said softly. 'I was completely forgetting about your marriage to Rachel. That was a good marriage, wasn't it?'

He nodded. 'But life moves on. You've helped to heal the wounds so that I could start again. And I know this time…'

'Richard, I have to think about it… I'm glad I've helped you, but you haven't known me very long. Now that you've found out what love is all about again you might want to play the field a bit before you settle down.'

'Darling Jane. You're the one I want to be with for the rest of my life.'

'It's like a dream,' she breathed. 'Any minute now I feel as if I'm going to wake up. But how long will the dream last? How long will it be before you tire of me, like all the other men in my life?'

Richard kissed her forehead, her eyes, her cheeks, her lips, before holding her against him as if he would never let her go.

'How can I convince you that I'm not like the other men in your life? People like Simon who was a philanderer, people like Paul who is incapable of loving anyone but himself...' He broke off and looked deep into her eyes. 'After all you've been through, it's not surprising you've lost the power to trust, Jane.'

'I know,' she said quietly. 'The past continues to haunt me. I've even prepared myself for the inevitable time when you will leave me.'

'I'm never going to leave you, Jane.'

What wonderful words! She had no doubt that Richard believed them now, but there was nothing to say that some time in the future, when she'd become inextricably tied to him, he wouldn't break her heart.

'Give me some time to think. It's all so unexpected,' she said.

Richard sighed as he pulled himself away and started up the car.

The Montgomery farm came into view as they crested the brow of the hill that overlooked Deepdale. The morning mist had cleared and the dale was flooded in bright sunshine. The sheep who had been brought down from the high ground were cropping the grass beside the river.

The sun was glinting on the windows as Richard drove through the gateway, coming to a halt by the kitchen door. His mother came out almost immediately.

'Sorry we're late, Mum,' Richard said, giving his mother a kiss on the cheek.

Sylvia moved across towards Jane and took hold of both her hands. 'It's lovely to see you again, Jane.'

Jane found the sincerity and warmth of her welcome very touching. Having an affair with Sylvia's son was one thing, but how would she react if she knew Richard had proposed? This only son, the apple of his parents' eye, a man who could have any girl he wanted but had made the unlikely choice of Plain Jane.

She put on her social smile. 'I'm glad to be here again.'

'Desmond's waiting in the dining room. I've got all the food keeping hot in my hostess trolley.'

Richard smiled. 'Rolling out the red carpet, eh? We would have settled for sandwiches in the kitchen, Mum.'

Sylvia gave him a conspiratorial glance. 'I like the chance to put on a show when we have a guest.'

'Jane!' Desmond rose from his carved wooden chair at the head of the table. 'How lovely to see you again. Come and sit here beside me.'

He was holding out her chair. As she sat down she noticed a couple of stains on her working skirt.

'I haven't had time to change since doing an emergency delivery this morning,' she said, quickly picking up the starched napkin beside her plate and covering the offending marks on her lap.

'You look charming, my dear,' Richard's father said. 'And thank you so much for writing to me. I was only too pleased to be able to help you.'

'I can't thank you enough for your help,' Jane said. 'As I told Richard, it was like having a huge weight taken from my shoulders.'

Desmond smiled. 'He deserved to get his comeuppance, that wretched Paul Drew! I don't like to hear about vulnerable women being taken for a ride.'

He paused, looking down the long refectory table as if checking that everyone was present and correct.

Jane felt a surge of affection for the older Montgomery man. He was well respected in his chosen profession. This is how Richard would be in a few years' time. But would she be sitting at the other end of his table after a lifetime of professional achievement and the raising of a family? Or would Richard have become restless somewhere along the line and asked her for a divorce? Or would she have played safe and remained single?

To remain single would be the easy, boring option. But to marry and risk being dumped at a later date…

'Now, can I help you to some of this pâté, Jane?' Desmond was saying. 'And there's salad further down the table on its way if Richard would do the honours.'

'What kind of an emergency did you say you had, Jane?' Sylvia asked, as she pushed the heavy wooden salad bowl from the end of the table towards Richard.

Richard picked up the wooden salad servers and passed them across to Jane. 'We delivered a baby, Mum.'

'Good heavens! I thought they were all born in hospital nowadays.'

'Some of them choose to arrive ahead of schedule,' Richard explained patiently.

Sylvia looked down the table at her captive audience. She loved having her family around her. Life could be so dull now that she hardly ever got any professional work.

'Actually, now I remember, you arrived earlier than expected, Richard. I remember I was due to start filming in a couple of months and I was dying to shed my load and get in shape again. I couldn't believe it when you obliged by—'

'Darling, I don't think Jane wants to hear that old story!' Desmond said.

Sylvia glared at him. 'Oh, but she does! I used to be fascinated when your mother told me all those old stories about when you were a child. In the early days anyway. I think it's important for a woman to know about the man she's going to be shackled to for the rest of her life, don't you, Jane?'

Jane swallowed the piece of pâté she was chewing and attempted a smile. This was exactly the sort of question she'd been dreading.

Richard's father, sensing her discomfort, sprang to her aid. 'Sylvia, you forget that we'd been formally engaged before my mother started indulging herself by telling the family secrets. I think you're jumping the gun a little.'

He looked down the table at his wife. 'What has Mrs Dawson put in our mystery trolley for a main course, my dear?'

Sylvia had turned bright red with embarrassment and seemed relieved to stand up and lean over the trolley.

'I'm just trying to find out. I think it's lamb…no, it's chicken. The vegetables may be a bit dried up but…'

Richard began helping his mother to lift out the dishes from the hostess trolley parked beside her.

'I'm no good at cooking,' Sylvia said, still flustered by her *faux pas*. 'But I do so love entertaining.'

The topics of conversation from this point ranged from the weather, the changes taking place in medical care and the possibility of improving the facilities for art and culture in the area.

Sylvia was once again in full conversational flight as she served the delicious apple crumble. As chairman of the Moortown Arts Society, she spoke with great feeling about how she would like to see more promotion of facilities for drama in the area.

Jane found her fascinating as she talked at great length about a subject which was close to her heart. And while the conversation was on neutral ground she had no need to worry about the problem she would have to deal with later.

Looking across the table at Richard, she could feel her pulses racing. It was unbelievable that he'd asked her to marry him! She longed with all her heart to say yes! To tell his wonderful, charming parents that she was going to be their daughter-in-law...so why couldn't she?

Why was this awful nagging voice inside her head telling her to hold back?

'I'll bring coffee outside into the garden,' Sylvia said, moving towards the dining-room door. 'There won't be many more days like this before the winter sets in.'

Jane stood up. Richard was standing behind her chair, ready to escort her into the garden. She smiled up at him and saw the questioning look in his eyes.

'I'll join you in a moment,' she said.

She walked along the corridor and found the downstairs cloakroom. She stared at her face over the wash-basin as she washed her hands. Her skin was shiny and devoid of the make-up she'd applied at the crack of dawn—well, second crack, anyway! Was it possible that Richard actually wanted to tie himself to her for the rest of his life?

On impulse she crossed the corridor and went into the high-ceilinged kitchen. 'Can I carry something out for you, Sylvia?'

Sylvia turned towards her and smiled. 'Thank you, Jane. I've got this tray ready with the cups. The cafe-tière's almost done.'

She reached across and touched Jane's arm. 'I'm sorry if I embarrassed you just now. I'd just assumed that—'

'It's OK,' Jane said, quickly. She sat down at the kitchen table. 'In actual fact, Richard has asked me to marry him.'

As soon as she'd said it she felt a sense of relief. It

was good to share a secret which was burning inside her, insisting on revealing itself.

'But that's wonderful!' Sylvia sat down opposite Jane and leaned forward to take hold of her hands. 'So I wasn't jumping the gun, was I?'

'I don't know,' Jane said carefully. 'It's so difficult to give Richard an answer.'

'But don't you love him? I know he loves you to distraction. He told me so.'

'Did he?' She caught her breath. 'And I love him, but...'

'So what's the problem?'

'I can't believe he'll want to stay with me for the rest of his life. And if he left me I would...'

'Ah!' Sylvia squeezed her hand. 'You know, marriage is all about trust. You just have to believe it will last and to work at it when it seems like crumbling a bit.'

She hesitated before continuing, 'You know, Richard told me you'd been let down by some difficult characters. That awful Simon! You couldn't have met a more unreliable person. Richard said he'd arranged a meeting between you so that you'd be able to shelve that problem and move on.'

'It certainly did help me,' Jane said quietly.

Sylvia smiled. 'Richard hoped it would...and then there was that dreadful scoundrel, Paul Drew! I know it meant a lot to Richard when Desmond agreed to sort out that problem. He said he thought it would help you come to terms with that unpleasant episode in your life.'

'Yes, it's got rid of a lot of subconscious bitterness,' Jane admitted.

Sylvia squeezed her hand. 'That was what Richard was hoping for.' She paused, her eyes searching Jane's face.

'There's just one little piece of the puzzle I don't under-stand…'

Jane looked up at her. 'What's that?'

Sylvia's eyes held a questioning expression. 'It's got something to do with that house that Paul Drew lived in. Someone bought it after it had been repossessed, but now it's on the market again. Richard was mad keen to buy it a few weeks ago. He told me he wanted you to visit it again, to lay the ghost of your unfortunate experiences there. Do you think it would? I can understand why you might hate the place…'

'I was very apprehensive at first, but now I can't wait to see it. In some indefinable way, I think that might be the key to unlocking my future.'

'I hope so…. You know, you mustn't think of Richard as being anything remotely like the men you've shared your life with before. I know he's longing to prove that you can trust him.'

'Thanks,' Jane said quietly. 'You've helped me a great deal.'

Sylvia gave her a broad smile. 'So shall I throw out the coffee and crack open the champagne?'

Jane stood up. 'Let's stick to coffee for the moment, but keep the champagne in the fridge, will you?'

She picked up the tray and carried it outside into the sunshine. The two men were engrossed in conversation about the state of farming in the area. Jane joined in, anxious to keep the conversation on neutral ground. She was well aware that Richard's mother was watching her.

It was wonderful to feel that she would be welcomed into this family if she really did take the plunge and quelled her doubts.

Richard put down his coffee-cup. 'I've got an appoint-ment with the estate agents in half an hour.'

Jane looked across at him questioningly.

'Would you like to look around Felldale, Jane, or shall I drop you off at Highdale?' he said quietly.

She sneaked a look at his mother as she stood up. Sylvia gave her a surreptitious wink.

'I'd love to see it,' she said firmly.

CHAPTER TEN

JANE barely recognised Felldale as Richard parked the car in the circular drive.

'It looks a lot more inviting than when I was last here,' she said, climbing out of the passenger seat. 'I could never understand why Paul didn't make some improvements. The paint was dark and peeling off everywhere, but look at it now!'

'Paul didn't intend to stay and, anyway, he didn't have any money to spare,' Richard said, taking hold of her hand. 'The people who bought it after it was repossessed made a lot of changes, as you'll see.'

She cried out in delight as she went from room to room, expressing her approval of the new, lighter decor. 'It's as if someone's taken the roof off and let the sunshine inside.'

He caught up with her and pulled her against him, holding her still. 'You can see why I fell in love with the place. And I wanted you to love it so that... Just wait until you see the bedrooms!'

Richard took her hand and led her up the wide, curving staircase. At the top she pulled away so that she could inspect every room, taking her time to soak up the new, welcoming atmosphere.

'Come and look at the master bedroom,' he called.

Jane felt suddenly shy as she joined him in the huge room that looked out over the front of the house.

'I wonder why the people left their bed?' she asked, moving across the room, mesmerised by the antique, wrought-iron bed that dominated one wall. 'It's gorgeous! I couldn't bear to be parted from this if it were mine.'

'Apparently, it was too big for the smaller home the people were moving to. The estate agents said it goes with the house.'

'I love it.' She sat down on the bed and began bouncing up and down. 'The mattress is so soft and...'

Richard sat down beside her and pulled her against him. 'You can't have the bed without the house,' he said in a gravelly voice. 'And you can't have the house without me, so what's your answer?'

Jane smiled up into his eyes as he pulled her back on to the mattress. 'I think I'll settle for the whole package.'

His kiss was, oh, so gentle as she gave up all resistance. For the first time she could see the future stretching ahead of her. Since she'd walked over the threshold of this wonderful, welcoming house, she'd finally felt that she could give Richard her implicit trust.

And just before his caressing hands took away all rational thought Jane was able to convince herself that it wasn't all a dream. The dream had finally turned into reality...

The sun was setting outside the curtainless windows as Jane opened her eyes. She shivered as she snuggled closer to Richard. He reached out and covered her naked body with his shirt and jacket.

'We've got half an hour before surgery,' he whispered.

She groaned. 'And it's my turn tonight.'

He kissed her gently on the cheek. 'Oh, no! I'm going to do it. You must be exhausted. I've got to take care of my future wife.'

She turned towards him, smiling. 'Your wife. I like the sound of that.'

Richard bent his head towards her. 'So do I,' he breathed, huskily, before covering her lips with his own.

He raised his head. 'I've known since the first couple of months that I wanted to marry you, but you were a daunting prospect.'

'Thanks very much!'

He gave her a rakish grin. 'You're completely unique, a combination of intelligence, wit, independent ideas…'

She laughed. 'You've forgotten to say I've got a face that would launch a thousand ships! I tried to change my appearance for you but—'

'Darling Jane, don't ever change! Promise me, you'll stay just as you are.'

'That's one promise that will be easy to keep. And before you start…Richard, I really think we should be going back to Highdale before…'

'Just one more kiss…'

EPILOGUE

WHAT a difference a year makes! Jane thought as she gently laid her baby son, Edward, back in his cot beside their huge wrought-iron bed. Tenderly, she smoothed back the tuft of blond hair that lay across his forehead. He'd watched her with wide, trusting, blue eyes as she'd fed him, but his eyes were now closed and he'd already drifted back into the deep untroubled sleep of childhood.

She turned to look at Richard, who also looked as if his sleep was deep and untroubled. The perfect family man! Who would have thought it all those years ago when she'd first known him as a carefree medical student?

A deep sense of peace stole over her as she lay back against her pillows and looked across at the pale light of dawn creeping through the window. The sun was peeping over the top of the fell, a tiny point of white light that quickly burst into a big round flame of fire. It was late September but the summer still lingered.

Jane loved these early mornings when she was alone with her husband and son, before the day really began. They always slept with the curtains open to remind them of their first time here in this room, when the dream had finally come true. She fingered the linen sheets she'd bought for their bed. They hadn't had sheets that day but they hadn't noticed. She was absolutely sure that had been when Edward had been conceived because that had been the first time that she and Richard had decided to dispense with contraception!

She snuggled closer to Richard. He murmured something in his sleep. She smiled. He looked so like his son, or was it that their son looked so much like him? Whatever! She loved them both as dearly but in a different kind of way.

Her mind wandered back over the eventful year since they'd lain on this bed, desperately trying to drag themselves away so that they could deal with the evening surgery and all the other duties that had had to be performed on that momentous evening.

She'd insisted they shared the evening surgery, and between each patient Richard had phoned through on the intercom to ask if she still loved him! And when one of the patients, sensing what was going on, had asked when they were going to get married Richard had willingly shared the secret. The joyful news had spread like wildfire!

She remembered the phone calls they'd made after surgery. Sylvia and Desmond had insisted on coming over to Highdale, complete with bottles of champagne, for an impromptu engagement party which had culminated in Jane and Richard having to put both their fathers to bed, very much the worse for drink! Desmond and Sylvia had slept in the guest bedroom that night. And after that riotous evening there had never been any doubt that the Montgomery and Crowther families would get on like a house on fire.

Even Caroline, who'd driven over in record time as soon as she'd received her phone call, had agreed that with a wedding in the offing their romance looked promising!

Their wedding, on the Saturday before Christmas, was idyllic. The snow arrived on the high fells the day before and obligingly scattered a few flakes on the church on the actual wedding day. It seemed as if the whole of Highdale and half of Moortown turned up for the event and most of them found their way over to Fellside for the reception.

Jane was already three months pregnant on their wedding day and hugging the joyful secret inside her. Richard knew, of course, and was finding it difficult to keep the wonderful news between them. She'd told him the moment the pregnancy test had been positive but she didn't announce the good news to everyone else until the spring. And then there were rapid arrangements to be made before the birth in June.

Ann, one of her old friends in the village, had given up nursing at Moortown before her two school-age children had been born. She didn't want a full time job but was happy to come over to Fellside most mornings and any other times when Jane's duties meant she needed her to look after Edward. Jane worked fewer hours at the surgery towards the time of the birth and Richard coped admirably with the extra workload. Once Edward was a month old she worked mornings at Highdale and took the occasional clinic.

Before she'd moved into Fellside, she'd offered the Highdale flat above the old stables to Maria, a young community nurse, and her husband, who'd promised to keep an eye on her father when neither she nor Richard were there. Her father seemed to get on extremely well with them and—which was equally important—Mrs Bairstow didn't object to Maria taking over her kitchen in the evening and cooking so they could all have supper together.

Richard was opening his eyes. He gave her a sexy, lazy smile and, drawing her against him, kissed her tenderly on the lips.

'Morning, darling. Why were you looking so solemn just now?'

Jane smiled. 'Was I? I wasn't feeling solemn. I was thinking about the past year.'

He laughed. 'What a difference a year makes!'

'Exactly! Just think. Almost a year to the day we were lying in this bed...'

'On this bed, you mean! As I remember, there was simply a mattress and I had to hold you so close to keep you warm that—'

'So you were simply keeping me warm, were you?'

'Mmm.' He caressed her bare shoulders. 'And you feel very cold now, so I think I should warm you again...'

A couple of hours later, she kissed his cheek. 'We really ought to get up. Edward's waking again and Ann will be here any minute. I should be showered and dressed and ready to leave.'

'You haven't got a clinic this afternoon, have you?'

'No, I'll be home all afternoon. Why?'

He gave her a rakish smile. 'So will I, with any luck. Would you have a date with me in the garden of the most beautiful house in Yorkshire?'

'Only if I can bring my baby...'

'How long did you say he sometimes sleeps in the afternoon...?'

MILLS & BOON®

Makes any time special™

Mills & Boon publish 29 new titles every month. Select from...

Modern Romance™   Tender Romance™

Sensual Romance™

Medical Romance™   Historical Romance™

MAT2

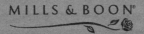

MILLS & BOON®

Medical Romance™

CLAIMED: ONE WIFE by Meredith Webber
Book two of The Australian Doctors duo

Neurosurgeon Grant Hudson knows that fraternisation between colleagues can break hearts, ruin careers and even lives. Yet for Dr Sally Cochrane, he is prepared to break his own rule. Sally, however, has her own reasons for keeping him out of her life...

A NURSE'S FORGIVENESS by Jessica Matthews
Book one of Nurses Who Dare trilogy

Marta Wyman is not going to let Dr Evan Gallagher pressurise her into meeting up with her grandfather. No matter how handsome, polite and charming Evan is he will have a long wait before she changes her mind— or gives in to her desires...

THE ITALIAN DOCTOR by Jennifer Taylor
Dalverston General Hospital

Resentment simmered between Luke Fabrizzi and Maggie Carr when her family tried to introduce them with marriage in mind. But a staged relationship in order to avert their families led to a truce—and another battle against their true feelings!

On sale 4th May 2001

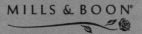

Medical Romance™

NURSE IN NEED *by Alison Roberts*

Emergency nurse Amy Brooks rushed into an engagement when she realised she wanted a family of her own—then she met Dr Tom Barlow. She had to end the engagement and Tom was delighted—but was his love for Amy the real reason?

THE GENTLE TOUCH *by Margaret O'Neill*

Jeremy is asked to persuade Veronica Lord into letting him treat her. Just as he gains her trust, Jeremy discovers that he was present when she had her accident and could have helped her. Will she ever be able to forgive him, let alone love him?

SAVING SUZANNAH *by Abigail Gordon*

Until Dr Lafe Hilliard found her, Suzannah Scott believed she had nothing left. Lafe helped her to rebuild her life and all he wanted in return was honesty. But if Suzannah revealed her past, she risked not only losing his professional respect, but his love…

On sale 4th May 2001

4 FREE

books and a surprise gift!

We would like to take this opportunity to thank you for reading this Mills & Boon® book by offering you the chance to take FOUR more specially selected titles from the Medical Romance™ series absolutely FREE! We're also making this offer to introduce you to the benefits of the Reader Service™—

- ★ FREE home delivery
- ★ FREE gifts and competitions
- ★ FREE monthly Newsletter
- ★ Exclusive Reader Service discounts
- ★ Books available before they're in the shops

Accepting these FREE books and gift places you under no obligation to buy, you may cancel at any time, even after receiving your free shipment. Simply complete your details below and return the entire page to the address below. *You don't even need a stamp!*

YES! Please send me 4 free Medical Romance books and a surprise gift. I understand that unless you hear from me, I will receive 6 superb new titles every month for just £2.49 each, postage and packing free. I am under no obligation to purchase any books and may cancel my subscription at any time. The free books and gift will be mine to keep in any case.

M1ZEA

Ms/Mrs/Miss/Mr ....Initials....................................
BLOCK CAPITALS PLEASE

Surname ....

Address ....

....

....Postcode...............................

Send this whole page to:
UK: FREEPOST CN81, Croydon, CR9 3WZ
EIRE: PO Box 4546, Kilcock, County Kildare (stamp required)